Also by Ken Baker

How I Got Skinny, Famous, and Fell Madly in Love
Fangirl

FINDING FOREVER

by Ken Baker

RP TEENS
PHILADELPHIA · LONDON

A *DEADLINE DIARIES* EXCLUSIVE

Books published by Running Press are available at special discounts for bulk purchases
in the United States by corporations, institutions, and other organizations. For more
information, please contact the Special Markets Department at the Perseus Books Group,
2300 Chestnut Street, Suite 200, Philadelphia, PA 19103, or call (800) 810-4145,
ext. 5000, or e-mail special.markets@perseusbooks.com.

ISBN 978-0-7624-5594-2
Library of Congress Control Number: 2015942597
E-book ISBN 978-0-7624-5817-2

9   8   7   6   5   4   3   2   1
Digit on the right indicates the number of this printing

Front cover image: Legs of woman in water © Thinkstock Images
Back cover image: Gold abstract background © Thinkstock Images/Milanares

Designed by T.L. Bonaddio
Edited by Lisa Cheng
Typography: Adobe Garamond, Akzidenz Grotesk, ITC Century,
DIN Schriften, Entypo, Museo Sans, Museo Slab, Courier,
Helvetica Neue, Officina, Ostrich, Trade Gothic, Univers

Published by Running Press Teens
An Imprint of Running Press Book Publishers
A Member of the Perseus Books Group
2300 Chestnut Street
Philadelphia, PA 19103–4371

Visit us on the web!
www.runningpress/rpkids

For Jackson Lawrence,
Chloe Brant, and
Kimberly Brooke,
whom I love three-slice

I'D RATHER DIE YOUNG FOR EXPOSING THE TRUTH THAN LIVE FOREVER FOR IGNORING IT.

BROOKLYN BRANT, Editor & Founder DeadlineDiaries.com

Birthday bliss. Taylor Prince pinched her eyes shut and punched her hands skyward, soaking in her final hours of being fifteen. Dancing on her packed pool deck, feeling the music, she shook off all the dramas that came with being a world-famous movie star.

Yet she didn't party recklessly—the last thing she wanted was to unravel the interlaced princess side braid that snaked down the side of her neck. The crisscross weave had taken her over an hour of mirror-assisted trial and error to get just right. Like nearly every style Taylor tried, she wore the hairdo well. Very well.

But as Taylor had long ago learned, looking great was usually a lot easier to achieve than feeling great.

Taylor did her best to ignore the stresses that consumed most party hostesses: *Is everyone having fun? . . . Will the late-night taco truck come on time? . . . Is my makeup holding up in the humidity? . . . Are the old-fart neighbors down the canyon going to call the cops again? . . . Will Evan make a surprise appearance and give me a much needed birthday kiss?*

Instead of worrying, she smiled, drew in a breath, and watched as the orange haze morphed into the kind of planetary purple that made So Cal sunsets the stuff of legend.

This is everything I dreamed of . . .

Being a celebrity meant saying yes to a lot of things she'd rather not do. But not on this Saturday night. Taylor had made it this far playing by the rules of the Hollywood fame game, and she believed she had finally earned the right to say:

No reporters.

No fans.

No agent.

No manager.

No publicist.

No party planner.

No bodyguards.

No directors.

No scripts.

No studio execs.

No cameras.

No Twitter.

No Snapchat.

No Instagram.

No worries.

No problems.

These were birthday desires that Taylor hoped would become a Sweet Sixteen dream.

"All rise."

Brooklyn Brant, who was by at least two decades the youngest of the worshippers scattered around the mostly empty church, followed Father McGavin's command and stood at her pew. After a brief prayer, she made the sign of the cross in front of her chest, sat down, and folded her hands in her lap.

"Now, a reading," the priest announced, "from the book of Job."

Brooklyn pulled a black paperback Bible from the bench slot in front of her. When she was a little kid, Brooklyn's bright-blue eyes had been known to close in the resting position (aka a mid-sermon nap). Her long, straw-straight red hair used to veil her eyes, but such clandestine snoozing could no longer go unnoticed since she now wore her bangs cut short.

But tonight Brooklyn wasn't bored. She did, however, lack the one thing she very much needed: direction. She had come seeking, wanting an answer . . . a message . . . a sign. Anything would do. From God. Maybe even from her late father.

Most *normal* sixteen-year-olds in Twin Oaks spent their Saturday nights doing things like going to movies, attending house parties, blowing their allowances on useless junk at Wal-Mart, obsessively stalking boys on social media, or even going on actual IRL dates. Not Brooklyn. Lately she almost always spent her Saturday evenings alone in church, usually followed by a late night hunched over her laptop updating her celebrity news blog, *DeadlineDiaries.com*. Though it meant some lonely nights, Brooklyn felt a sense of pride in being anything but normal.

Taylor sparkled. Acting coaches had taught her to use her body as an instrument, and she was playing it. Silver body glitter shimmered on her chest, which was severely exposed by the plunging neckline of her maxi dress. Her hair swayed as her spiked heels scraped the patio to the rhythm of the beat.

Flirty dancing in a dramatic black dress was the most scandalous thing about Taylor this evening. Despite the rumors, Taylor didn't drink alcohol or do drugs—or sleep around. She'd only had one boyfriend—ever. And the only thing she snorted was the occasional silly laugh that emanated from her narrow nose, which, according to a press release from the Association of Plastic and Cosmetic Surgeons, had become the most sought-after by young women going in for nose jobs this past year.

Taylor had seen the roadkill of former child stars flattened by fame. Substance-abuse sloppiness, an arrest, court-ordered rehab and/or community service, a redemptive PR campaign. Then, in some cases, a career comeback. The meltdown cycle had become a rite of passage, but Taylor had vowed not to fall into that trap.

She couldn't, however, control what the media spread. *Taylor Prince's Diva Demands Fit for a Queen! . . . Taylor Prince's Royal Drug Problem!*

Taylor had five blockbuster movies, too many magazine covers to count, a namesake clothing line and fragrance, a Golden Globe, a BAFTA, and an Oscar nomination. She had an agent and a manager who signed on after she made it big from the YouTube casting reel she uploaded when she was in middle school, and she had her mom, who was now back in

Arizona caring for her little sister—a fact her phone reminded her of when it bleeped alive.

> Happy birthday, tay! Penny and I wish we
> could be there! XO—mommy

But before Taylor could tap out a reply, *he* appeared.

Boyish grin framed by scruffy five o'clock shadow.

Retro-style Ray-Bans that matched his buzz-cut dark hair.

A white T-shirt that likely covered up a sexy six-pack.

Faded blue jeans were draped casually from just below his hips, held up by a thick brown belt that coordinated perfectly with his weathered cowboy boots.

Intricate sleeves of tattoos twisted around his taut forearms.

He reminded Taylor of the kind of guy whose pictures she used to cut out of magazines and tape onto her bedroom wall when she was, say, eleven. Or fifteen. Or, apparently, just minutes from turning sixteen.

A cross. The silver necklace dangled from her neck.

Brooklyn lifted the tiny crucifix and kissed it before starting her silent prayer. She didn't come for help coping with the mean girls who called her a nerd, a loner, an emo, and worse. She heard the snickers in the hall about her wearing her boyish T-shirts and favorite L.A. Kings hat every day. She saw the Instagram posts from parties her supposed friends hadn't invited her to.

No, she had long ago opted to focus on decidedly more adult-ish concerns, namely *DeadlineDiaries.com*.

Rather than just breaking the Big Three of celebrity "soft" news (hookups, breakups, and personal life screw-ups) that populated most Hollywood-focused websites and blogs, Brooklyn had a nose for harder news—castings, on-set gossip, contract negotiations, box office projections, script leaks, and studio and network insider gossip. She regularly published exclusives on the hottest young celebrities. But trying to compete with experienced bloggers and corporate media sites brimming with professional staff reporters and editors and photo budgets beyond her reach was at best daunting, and at worst entirely demoralizing.

Brooklyn liked that no one bothered her at Saturday night Mass. No well-intentioned neighbors assuring Brooklyn that she remained in their prayers. No leering looky-loos sneaking their puppy-dog glimpses at poor, fatherless Brooklyn Brant. And without the pressure to come looking her Sunday best, she could worship comfortably alongside the mostly senior citizen congregation in her favorite jeans and sneakers. She always showed respect by taking off her baseball cap and placing it next to her on the pew.

To Brooklyn, the Bible could be a lot like the juiciest tabloid stories—filled with a lot of truth, insight, drama, and useful information, but not necessarily a 100-percent-accurate historical record. Nor did it espouse a belief system without its flaws when put through her modern-day, post-feminist lens. Brooklyn approached religion with the same take-the-good-with-the-bad philosophy that her father had taught her. As he often would say, "Don't throw the Bible out with the bathwater."

Here she could focus solely on the centering sensation she got from spending an hour just being alone, listening to the priest, praying to God, looking for inspiration that might motivate and inspire. She also enjoyed the moments of silence that allowed her to talk to her dad.

She realized the notion that she and her father could communicate with each other sounded a little "out there." Which is partly why she didn't like to talk about it. But the voice she often heard, though silent, was real and strong and unmistakably her father's. Calm. Direct. Honest. Helpful. Caring. And when necessary, even bossy.

It helped that Father McGavin, though pushing seventy, wasn't some out-of-touch old bag of Bibles.

"In the book of Job, we meet a young man named Elihu," Brooklyn's lifelong priest began. "Elihu grew frustrated being the 'young' guy, listening to the supposedly wiser elders arguing. So he stood up and really laid into the old men." The priest flipped the heavy Scripture page. "It is not only the old who are wise, not only the aged who understand what is right."

Blip, BLIP! Blip, BLIP! Blip, BLIP!

The congregation turned their attention to the redhead in the fourth row from the rear. One lady craned her neck and barked a "shush."

Brooklyn fumbled to find her blipping phone as Father McGavin paused and cleared his throat.

Holy . . . Brooklyn's face grew hot as she fished into her pocket in a panic.

Blip, BLIP! Blip, BLIP!

Finally she clicked the phone silent and squeezed the device between her thighs.

"Sorry," she said, pressing her palms together and shrugging.

A minute later, once peace and worshipful order had been restored, Brooklyn snuck a glance at her text alert.

Pizza later?!

Brooklyn tapped out a reply.

Ugh, Holden. I'm @ church, duh!

so is that a yes?

OK. Fine. Make it thin crust, pepperoni

A pizza order wasn't exactly the kind of "sign" from God that Brooklyn had been looking for, but at least she wouldn't be spending Saturday night alone.

"For you." Pretty Boy flashed Taylor a dimpled smile. "Drink up."

Taylor took a swig from the red plastic cup he gave her. Tasting the bitterness, she swallowed hard, pushing the syrupy liquid down her throat and into her stomach, where it settled warmly. She licked her lips and took another gulp, emptying the cup but for a few lonely ice cubes at the bottom.

Taylor turned her back to Pretty Boy and raised her arms straight up, showing off some booty popping of the kind she'd seen in those crazy Juicy J dance videos.

Stop talking and start twerking, babyyyy.

Taylor had always pegged guys who wore sunglasses at night as little more than pretentious posers, narcissistic to the point of making themselves entirely unattractive to her. But she decided this particular piece of human hotness was far too hot to judge solely by his cover.

The incandescence of the Milky Way shimmered above, while below, the steep canyon gave way to the L.A. basin and the city lights that shined just as brightly. Taylor stopped dancing mid-song and pulled out her cell, which she had expertly tucked into the tight-fitting chest of her dress.

She texted her assistant, Simone, who danced on the other side of the patio.

So is he my secret bday present u promised?

Um, yeah . . .

Taylor looked up from her screen just long enough to lock eyes briefly with Simone. A nod and smile.

Taylor wished most Hollywood guys who hit on her looked

as hot as Pretty Boy. But sadly, they didn't. Pimple-faced fan boys with crushes. Creepy old guys. Vain actors. Stoners. Fame seekers. And perhaps most unappealing were the paparazzi rats who camped outside her house on the hunt.

A Tae Kwon Do black belt since the age of eleven, Taylor had been known to groin-kick paps, causing major headaches for her publicist, Amanda, who liked to remind her that rude photogs were just another "price of fame." At those moments, Taylor wanted a refund.

Taylor snuck a glimpse at Pretty Boy, who still hadn't taken his gaze off her. She looked directly at him with an expressionless supermodel stare.

Taylor's unspoken truth: she wished Evan Ryan were the one making the moves on her. Evan had co-starred alongside her in the romantic comedy *Final Verse*, where they (rather convincingly) played boyfriend and girlfriend. Taylor had suffered a class-A crush on Evan from the first day of shooting, and it only got more intense after many, many, *many* make-out scenes.

Taylor decided that once their movie wrapped, Evan would be her First.

Nearly a year later, it hadn't happened. That's why he was the first person she invited to her party. A few days later, Evan had called, telling her he would love nothing more than to celebrate her birthday, but, sadly, he couldn't make it. Avoiding any place that might have alcohol or drugs, he said, was part of his "recovery" following his recent stint in rehab. Taylor promised she would make it a clean party, and Evan said he would consider it.

"Three minutes!" Simone shouted, the crowd responding with a chorus of "woots" as they toasted their cups. Taylor went in to slap Simone a high five, but she missed. Sloppily.

"Happy b-day, T!" Simone stuck her arms straight out, gripping an imaginary steering wheel of the Range Rover Taylor looked forward to cruising once she got her license. "Drive time, baby!"

Another up-tempo remix delivered the soundtrack of Taylor's mating movie. Taylor felt the first hand rest firmly above her right hipbone, sending a shiver across her lower back that exploded downward into her thighs as he gripped tighter. Then came the other hand from behind, firmly connecting to her left hip. Taylor didn't flinch. Instead, she rolled with the music as Pretty Boy's strange but warm hands guided her body.

Side to side. Front to back. Up and down. Taylor hadn't felt male hands on her like this since she and Evan had sort of hooked up right before he left for rehab. This boy was Trouble. And she loved it.

Midnight came in a blur as the party people—except for Pretty Boy, whose hands were occupied on Taylor's waist—raised their cups and sang "Happy Birthday."

"Welcome to sixteen," Pretty Boy whispered, his scruff gently scraping her cheek. Taylor pressed her back tightly against his chest, the top of her head fitting perfectly beneath his chin.

His words came off his lips with a yogi-like calm.

Sixteen . . .

His voice could just . . . *lull* . . . *her* . . . *to* . . . *sleep*.

The frenetic party suddenly went slo-mo. Taylor managed to turn around and face Pretty Boy. To brace for the face-plant she felt coming, she leaned forward and pressed her cheek against his upper chest, wrapping her arms around him.

Looking around his tricep, she saw a blurry vision of two men with guns drawn, bursting through the side yard gate.

The music abruptly stopped. A few girls shrieked. More than a few others dropped f- and s-bombs.

The crowd dispersed like a busted protester mob, scattering in all directions—back inside the house, hopping over the short fence, darting out the side gate and beelining it to their cars.

Taylor stood in shock beside the pool, clawing Pretty Boy's muscled back. She looked down into the deep end, her arms feeling like barbells while she was unable to move anything except for her stiffening neck. When she managed to glance behind her, no one was there. The shouting men with the guns across the pool, she realized, were, in fact, coming after her.

"Hands up!"

The sound of rushing air forcing in and out of her lungs muted the shouting.

"Hands up!" the man ordered again. "Pour out your drinks and leave the property. Now!"

Taylor tried blinking away her blurry focus, but she could barely move her eyelids.

Her dance partner wrapped his arms tightly around her and whispered, "It's tiiiiime."

And everything—including the glowing Milky Way matrix—faded to black.

Brooklyn laughed. "You're totally punking me."

"I'm not—this is real." The caller's voice cracked with desperation. "I really do need your help."

"Okay, I believe you." Brooklyn sighed. "But I'm just a blogger, not Google."

No giggle. Not even a courtesy "ha-ha" from the chick.

Just. Awkward. Silence.

Unless she was in church, Brooklyn didn't readily embrace moments of empty ear space.

"Just kidding. You know, totally J-K. I don't specialize in—"

"I know exactly what you do," the anonymous girl said. "I've been reading your blog, like, forever. I know that if anyone can help me, it's *you*."

"That's very nice of you. But what kind of help are you talking about?"

"The kind where you help me find somebody."

"Find who?"

"It's . . . I can't say. Not yet. Sorry, um . . ."

Brooklyn grunted. "Have you asked Siri? She's so much smarter with the upgrade."

"I wish. This person—this *special* person—well, to be honest with you, she's basically gone missing."

"Hey, it's a *she*!" Brooklyn said. "Actual info! Now we're making some progress. And you're lucky it's a girl, because I know far less about where boys like to hide out."

"That's the thing—she's not hiding. She hasn't gone away on her own. She was taken."

Brooklyn rolled her eyes in a way she was too polite to do face-to-face. "Do you know she was taken away or do you just assume she was? Because one of the most basic rules of investigative journalism is to assume nothing, verify everything. There's a saying that when you assume anything all you do is make an *ass* out of *you* and *me*."

"This is a special person, Brooklyn."

"Wait. Special?"

"Yes," the caller said. "Very."

"Okay, but to be clear—and please don't take this the wrong way—do you mean disabled kind of *special*, or just, you know, a special person to you?"

"Special to a lot of people, Brooklyn."

"If she's so special, then maybe you better just call the cops."

"Brooklyn. . . . It's really not that simple."

Brooklyyyn . . . realaaay . . . simpuhl. The lazily drawn out back ends of words always gave away that Hollywood Girl twang. It suggested a person who got more manis and pedis than the usual girl. It suggested someone who did so using Daddy's AmEx. In Twin Oaks, most girls talked with an accent that sounded more hick than Hollywood. Twin Oaks didn't look far from L.A. on a map, but the city of 55,000 people surrounded by avocado and nut farms and oil fields in many ways had more in common with, say, Kansas than California.

"Just trying to help," Brooklyn said. "Cops find missing people, right? But that's not what I do. I cover celebrities. I break news. I'm not a detective."

Brooklyn got tweets every day from readers, most of whom she answered with a polite thank-you. Most asked for a link to their blogs or to follow them on Twitter. Or they just wanted to know where they could meet a certain star or whether some random rumor they'd heard was true.

Some tipsters, though, offered "actionable leads"—gossip, photos, or other tidbits of information that she could report on. Brooklyn treated every tip seriously, even if the tipster turns turned out to be a total flake. Which happened a lot.

This current caller claimed in her email last night to have a scoop she could not share over the computer because it was "too sensitive."

"Listen," Brooklyn said. "I can't help you if you can't even tell me who exactly you're looking for. So I'm going to have to just say thanks for reading my blog, I appreciate you thinking of me, but let's just call it a—"

"No, wait! Please. Don't hang up. You're the only person who can find her. I mean, the cops could, I guess. But they can't know everything. I just need you to do it."

"So you're telling me some *special* person is missing, but you won't tell me her name, or anything about her for that matter. You're afraid to go to the police for some unspecified sketch reason, and come to think of it, I don't even know who the hell *you* are. Put yourself in my shoes. How am I supposed to take you seriously?"

"The thing is . . . Can I trust you to keep this secret? Between us?"

"Sources come to me with scoops all the time." Though this was the first time anyone had ever called Brooklyn with what amounted to a missing person's report. "And I never, ever would burn a source."

"Okay, okay." The tipster exhaled. "It's a girl. And, um, you actually know who she is."

Brooklyn perked to attention. She stopped typing. "Okay. Go ahead . . ."

"It's Taylor Prince."

"Hold on. Let me get this straight, *the* Taylor Prince?"

"Unfortunately, yes."

"She's missing?"

"For the last two days."

"No offense," Brooklyn said, "but this could be a load of lies. In the last few years, there has hardly been a day when I didn't know where Taylor was. And my sources have already told me she's supposed to be taking a birthday vacation in Mexico. In my world, being MIA in Mexico doesn't qualify as 'missing.' It qualifies as being on vacation."

"She *was* supposed to head to Cabo yesterday, but that never happened."

"Bull."

"I'm sorry?"

"B-U-L-L," Brooklyn spelled out. "You know, as in you're full of it."

"Listen, I can assure you that I am definitely not—"

Brooklyn spit out a laugh. "Wait! Is this Tamara? Oh my god. It *is* Tamara! You almost got me!"

"Tamara?"

Brooklyn slapped her knee. "You got me *again*. You even perfected your Valley Girl voice—"

"I'm not Tamara—my name's Simone. And I really wish I was kidding. But I'm not."

"So, *Simone*, how exactly do you know Taylor Prince is missing?"

"Because I am close to her. Very close. I was with her when it happened."

"Wait, you're Simone *Witten*?"

"Yep," she said.

Brooklyn pushed her ear buds further in. She sat up straight.

"That's why I know so much about you," Simone said. "Taylor and I will be on a set or something, and before we even get out of her trailer to shoot the first scene, you will have pics of her on your site, plus a detailed schedule for the entire day. You're good at what you do, Brooklyn. Scary. But good."

Brooklyn still didn't feel convinced. Everyone knew that Taylor's longtime personal assistant and BFF was the tall, blonde Simone Witten. Simone sat beside her boss at awards shows, was thanked in her acceptance speeches, and shadowed Taylor virtually non-stop.

"How do I know you're not some weirdo?" Brooklyn asked.

"I get it," Simone said. "Working for a celebrity, I see a lot of oddballs. But honestly, the last twenty-four hours have been the craziest of my life. And I don't want to waste your time—or, more importantly, Taylor's. . . . You know, I can come meet you in person if that would make you feel better."

Brooklyn knew her worrywart mom would ground her for life for meeting up alone with a total stranger—especially one who had reached out to her from the blog making some pretty out-there claims. But what if Taylor Prince really had gone missing? It would be Brooklyn's biggest scoop yet, sending her number of daily unique visitors to over a million and putting her on the map with the big kahunas of Hollywood blogs—all just in time for the journalism school applications she had to start filling out next summer.

"Come meet me at the Frontier Valley High stadium," Brooklyn said. "Tomorrow morning at ten thirty."

"Where's that?" Simone asked.

"I'll text you the address. And then if you are for real, we can start."

"Start what?"

"The investigation."

Straps squeezing . . .

Black.

Hands pressing down on arms and legs . . .

Black.

Prick of the left arm with a needle . . .

Black.

Sharp pain on the right ankle . . .

Black.

Buzzing.

Black.

Spitting strands of hair from a cotton-dry mouth . . .

Black.

A scream . . .

Black.

"Go back to sleep, Taylor. You need your rest."

Black.

"Double it. Take her deeper!"

Black.

Brush teeth. Wash face and hands. Brush hair. Organize bathroom counter.

Make that *reorganize* every single item in the bathroom.

Brooklyn placed the plastic hairbrush on the far right side of the second drawer down (facing forward). Then she put her toothbrush, the pink one, on the right side of the sink about four inches from the wall, perfectly perpendicular to the mirror. (One time—just once—she had used a protractor to measure that the brush indeed was set at a 90-degree angle.) She folded the pink hand towel exactly in half and hung it over the silver rack on the wall. She opened and closed the drain of the sink four times, making sure it wasn't clogged, and turned both the hot and cold handles all the way to the right, mumbling "right is tight" with each fitful twist. Then came the toilet paper roll, which she spun into proper position: four squares dangling free.

Her mom once came home from Costco with a generic roll—not the usual Cottonelle two-ply—that had individual sheets just 3.8 inches long, rather than the standard 4.5 inches, which Brooklyn considered unacceptable. Her mom rolled her eyes, but she complied, returning later that day with rolls that had more suitable dimensions.

Brooklyn checked her watch. Exactly four minutes later, with everything in proper placement—including but not limited to the faucet handles of the shower turned to the same tightness and the shower stall door fully closed and the pink rug placed in the room's geometric center—Brooklyn could now leave home and head to her meeting at the school track.

A clear Southern California morning. Brooklyn leaned back on the bleachers, interlocking her hands behind her neck, sunning her freckled cheeks, counting any objects in her sight that she could group into fours. Four fence poles. Four white lines circling the track. Four rows of seats. Four cars passing by on El Camino Boulevard. Then she counted her breaths in fours.

Then she waited. And waited. And waited some more.

Brooklyn reasoned the Vitamin D production from the sun would be good for her. Even better, *D* was the fourth letter of the alphabet.

But now it was 11:04 a.m. and "Simone" was more than half an hour late.

Brooklyn set her phone's timer for four minutes. Her just-friend Holden sat in a patch of grass across the field. As she had instructed, his hand was ready to dial 911 the second "Simone" turned into a creepy kidnapper with ropes, knives, and a sack perfectly sized for a five-foot-four-inch blogger.

Holden didn't know about Simone, only that she was just the latest kind of anonymous tipster he had grown used to hearing Brooklyn talk about. After being snapped at countless times for even inquiring, Holden had learned not to ask anything about her confidential sources. Sources are to a news-breaking blogger what water is to a plant: Everything but the sun.

Just when the timer was about to go off, a lanky blonde in cutoff jeans and a tank top appeared across the stadium parking lot. She looked far older than a high school kid. And by the time the girl reached the bleachers, Brooklyn could see that she did, in fact, look exactly like the Simone Witten in paparazzi pictures.

Brooklyn slipped her cap back on, hopped down the four rows to the bottom, and feigned nonchalance with a laconic wave.

"Sorry, I'm so late," Simone said as she extended her right hand. "It's been a crazy couple days."

"It's okay." Brooklyn wiped the sweat off her palm before reciprocating. "Thanks for coming up. I know it's kind of far."

"No worries, but, yeah, I hardly ever get this far north of L.A. The 101 was a total parking lot. It took me almost two hours."

Brooklyn stopped herself from reminding Simone that a scene in Taylor Prince's movie *Girl on the Verge* was shot just two miles away, lest Simone think she was too much of a celeb stalker. "Twin Oaks is so far out of L.A. it might as well be Utah."

"You know, you're way prettier than I imagined," Simone said.

"Really? Were you expecting a hideous beast or something?"

"No, no, no. It's just that you don't have pictures of yourself on your blog and, well, most bloggers I've seen don't have gorgeous strawberry hair."

"Oh, this here mop?" Brooklyn grabbed a fistful of hair. "It's actually red. I'm a ginger."

Simone stood on the track with her arms wrapped around herself like it was 40, not 70, degrees. "I didn't mean to offend."

"Don't worry. I get that a lot. People always think I must be the weirdest little troll because I don't post selfies like the rest of the narcissistic world."

"Ahhh. So that's why you hardly ever post on Instagram."

"Honestly, I just want the focus to be on the stories and on the celebs, not on me. Maybe if more journalists had the same philosophy we'd all be a little better for it."

"Makes sense." Simone released her hands from around her arms. "Taylor doesn't even really like to do the whole social media thing, but she realizes it's for the fans. She usually has me post stuff for her."

"So you're the one who takes those Instagrams of her?"

"Yep. Usually. I'm the filter queen. Mayfair brings out the tan, Willow hides the pimples. The things you learn when you're an assistant . . ."

"You do all her tweeting, too?"

"Some of it, but not all. Taylor barely knows how to turn on her phone. But she's a brilliant actress and loyal person, which is why I love her." Simone smiled for the first time. "She's very dedicated to acting. When she's prepping for a role, she totally immerses herself into it. Like a thousand percent. Social media is just a distraction."

"That's why *I* love her," Brooklyn said.

Simone sighed. "I know you are a big fan, and you've always been a supporter, but do you really think you can help find her?"

"Yeah, I do think I can help. But I will need *a lot* more information from you. We can't play that guessing game like last night."

"I get it. I didn't drive two hours up here for nothing. I just had to make sure I could trust you. But I don't even know where to begin."

"You can start by telling me everything about that night," Brooklyn said, opening up a new Notes page on her phone. "And seriously, I mean *everything*."

Taylor blinked. The white morning light had never seemed so bright. She kept blinking until her eyes adjusted.

Buh-boom.

Her skull ached, the pain radiating from the back of her head out to each of her temples.

Buh-boom.

Flat on her back, she struggled to tuck her chin to her chest so she could see past her feet, out the window beyond her bed. She saw a grove of palm trees planted on a meticulously manicured green lawn, a jagged brown mountain peak littered with cactus and boulders. There wasn't a cloud in the sky and the only sound was the muted tweeting of sparrows from the grapefruit trees just outside her window.

A lounge chair sat in the far corner to her left, white with an orange accent pillow. A painted green metal door was on the right. A white desk beside the door, a green-and-white tile floor. Next to her bed rested a small nightstand, on which sat a lamp and a green plastic cup filled with water.

But no phone.

The room exhibited the spare elegance of a posh, if overly green-themed, hotel room. The sheets felt soft and cozy, and the modern furniture looked right out of an interior-decorating magazine. A tiny bathroom with a shower stall, sink, and toilet was to her left.

This was not the Four Seasons.

A woman in a white smock and dark green nurse pants walked into the room, rolling a cart with medical equipment.

"Where am I?" Taylor asked, still groggy.

"In a very safe, loving place," the woman calmly replied in

a thick Mexican accent. Lifting a blood pressure cuff from the cart, she secured it around Taylor's upper left arm. "That's the most important thing. You're safe here."

The machine beeped, releasing air from the cuff. The nurse glanced up at the digital screen and smiled politely.

"Seriously, where am I?" Taylor asked again.

"In very good hands."

"When did I get here?" Taylor struggled to recall her last memory. The pretty boy . . . the dancing . . . midnight . . . ?

"Ms. Prince," the woman said. "It's been at least a couple of days."

Taylor peeked under the blanket and saw she was wearing silk pajamas. But she didn't even own silk pajamas! In fact, she hated silk, the way it slid off her skin. And green? Little girls wore green PJs. Not to mention the fact that grandmas, not teens, wore silk "casualwear."

"Seriously, tell me right now. Please! This is so not okay. Where's my phone?"

The nurse placed her warm hand on Taylor's forehead and pressed firmly enough to guide her back down to the pillow. "Now, now . . ."

Taylor feared the woman was going to stick her with one of the needles resting on top of the cart. But a needle prick never came.

Instead the door clicked, unlocked. Pulling it ajar, the nurse added, "Sorry to be the one to tell you this, but you're in rehab."

And that news stung even more than a needle.

"So," Brooklyn said, "the cops crash the birthday party and then you—and basically everyone else except for Taylor—bolt?"

"It went down exactly like that," Simone said. "The cops came with their guns out and everything. And since almost everyone was under twenty-one, we all bailed. Out of instinct. I thought Taylor would talk her way out of it like she always does. But do I feel guilty for leaving her? Yes."

"I'm sorry, but I really don't get it. Why would the police have their guns out if they were just breaking up some teenager's party? Seems a little excessive to me. Plus, if it were a big enough deal for flashing guns, why would they just let everyone leave?"

"I don't know, but it must've been a raid or something."

"Exactly!" Brooklyn said.

"Exactly what?"

"A raid. Maybe the cops were tipped off about drugs and were looking for a particular person."

Simone shrugged. "Maybe."

"Was anyone doing drugs?"

"I don't know. Probably. Why's that matter?"

"Because, as everyone knows, cops love busting celebs. They like to make an example of them so that normal, everyday people will be afraid it could happen to them. So were they LAPD or, like, county sheriffs or some sort of security?"

"LAPD, I guess?"

"But you don't know for sure?"

"No, I really don't. Sorry."

"That's okay," Brooklyn said. "It's just that if they were some sort of private security, there wouldn't be a public record of their activity. But if they were cops, there should be a record of the raid that we can request. If it was FBI, which is possible, maybe I will file a FOIA."

"Foya?"

"Freedom of Information Act. It's a law that lets you access any federal records—like an FBI report—unless there is some national security reason for them to deny it. California, luckily, has a similar law for state agencies. We might be able to get the police reports if there are any."

"How do you know so much about this stuff?" Simone asked.

"My mom says that I have the equivalent of a PhD in investigative journalism. Self-taught, mostly. It's my passion."

"That's so funny."

"Funny how?"

"It's funny because Taylor always says if she ever goes to college she'll study journalism."

The revelation that Taylor fantasized about being a *journalist* qualified as major breaking news, the kind of story Brooklyn would normally turn into a splashy headline—EXCLUSIVE: TAYLOR PRINCE'S COLLEGE DREAM REVEALED!— which would definitely yield more than 100,000 page views, thus, generating more advertising revenue that she could tuck away into her college savings account. But today she realized she was chasing down much bigger, more important news that could put her on the journalism map so that Columbia and USC would be begging *her* to attend.

"So you didn't know these guys?" Brooklyn asked. "They weren't her security or something?"

"They acted—and looked—like cops," Simone said. "But I guess they could be FBI. They had on uniforms and stuff."

"Describe them."

"Definitely black pants. And black T-shirts."

"And how many guys were there?"

"Oh, umm. At least two. Yeah, two."

"And you're sure they wore black."

"Definitely," Simone answered. "I'm really good with clothes. I can forget people's names the second I meet them, but when it comes to fashion, I have a photographic memory."

"Well, if they wore black, they weren't County Sheriffs because they wear khaki shirts and green pants. And they weren't LAPD because they have blue, traditional uniforms. Plus cops don't usually wear T-shirts. And exactly where were *you* when they stormed into the backyard?"

"By the pool, across from Taylor. That part is all a little bit foggy, to be honest."

"Why? Were you drunk?"

"Um, yeah, maybe a tad."

"When do you turn twenty-one?"

"Next year. I can't wait."

Simone squinted at the far side of the fake stadium turf. She whispered, "I think we're being watched."

"Yeah. I *know* we are."

"You knew we were being watched this entire time?"

"That's not anyone important. Just my friend, Holden."

"Wait, so he knows about me? But you promised no one would know that I—"

"Calm down," Brooklyn said. "He doesn't know who you are, just that you are 'a source.' I had to have someone come here for my safety. I'm sure you can understand that. And since I'm not Taylor Prince, I don't have a bodyguard. Come to think of it, why didn't Taylor have any bodyguards?"

"She usually does, but she wanted to feel normal on her birthday so she had me send them home." Simone continued to eye Holden.

Brooklyn texted Holden.

Dude, all good here. Just go. Ur freaking
her out.

U sure?

Yes! Go. Ill txt ya later

Brooklyn put her phone down on the bleachers. "Holden's a real good guy. He's probably the biggest computer genius at school and loyal to a fault."

"You're dating?" Simone asked.

"No," she said. "But we've been kind of off and on since freshman year. Currently we are off."

"Why?"

"It's complicated."

Simone laughed. "Now you're the one playing coy."

"Honestly, I'm not. I just think of him more like a friend, a real good friend. My best friend. But he wants more."

"Bad kisser, huh?"

"No! Not at all. I mean, he's fine. It's just, well, you know, I don't need relationship drama. I don't think I could live without him, but high school sweethearts always break up, and it's usually ugly. It's cleaner this way. Safer."

"He obviously likes you," Simone said. "Coming here and all. And I don't blame him for liking you. And by the way, I love your bangs. I've always wanted to go short, but I'm too chicken to try."

"Short bangs are practical. No hair in my face. When you spend as much time as I do hunched over a laptop, you come to appreciate a she-mullet."

"Short hair, don't care?" Simone joked.

Brooklyn giggled. "Yep! Work in front, party in the back!"

Brooklyn knew that connecting on a personal level with sources could get them to open up more, but she also knew that few journalists ever broke a story by talking about their hairdos.

"You know," Brooklyn said, "don't feel guilty about leaving the party without her. Most people would have bolted. That's why I don't understand why Taylor didn't. Was she wasted or something?"

"Taylor doesn't drink or do drugs," Simone said. "Swear to God. Taylor has always been sober as a saint."

"Yes, rehab." The nurse repeated the news to Taylor when she returned for the second hourly checkup. "But clinically speaking, this is more than just a rehab. It's a center for rejuvenation. You'll see. It will transform you."

"But I don't drink or do drugs," Taylor said. "You guys know that, right? There has to have been some major misunderstanding, which I'm sure we can very easily straighten out." She pushed herself to sitting on her bed. "Now if you just let me call my assistant . . ."

The nurse pressed her hand down on top of Taylor's. "I'm sorry, dear. But you have here the leading specialists in the world of addiction and spiritual psychology. They will help you heal. You will get through this stage soon enough."

"Stage?"

"Denial," the nurse answered unemotionally. "It's just a stage. It will pass. Takes time. Part of the process."

Taylor scanned the room. She noticed a lens the size of an eyeball mounted into the corner above the door. "What's that?"

"A camera for your security. And safety."

"You are lying!" Taylor fully expected someone to barge into her room any moment and announce she was being filmed on a hidden camera TV show. "You're joking, right? You must be kidding me. This is *not* real."

The nurse pursed her lips, scribbling into a notebook. Taylor stood on the mattress, extended her hands toward the ceiling, and trampoline-bounced in an effort to grab the camera.

"Ms. Prince, I'd recommend you just lay back down. You've been through so much already." The nurse looked up from her notepad. "You really need your rest."

"With all due respect, you don't know what the hell you're talking about." Taylor sat down. "Just let me call my mom or my assistant!"

The nurse stared blankly back at her.

"Don't just stand there," Taylor added. "Get me a phone so I can get this straightened out!"

The nurse's expression turned grim, fearful. She stepped backward toward the door and pressed the buzzer on the wall. The door unlocked. "The doctor will be right with you," she said, opening the door and stepping out. "You can discuss this with him."

Taylor lunged to catch the heavy metal door before it closed, but just missed the handle before it snapped shut, the electric zap sounding as it locked. She pulled on the handle. When it didn't budge, she yanked it harder with both hands. Taylor pounded on the door and started screaming for them to open it. Whoever was "them."

"Please, return to bed," a male voice said sternly from a speaker built into the wall. "The doctor will be right with you. There is no need for alarm."

Taylor darted toward the room's only window and traced the outline of the square frame with her fingers looking for a latch.

There was none.

Taylor clutched her head in frustration, reaching for a fistful of hair. But her hands only slipped through. She pulled frantically several times, then patted and clawed all around her scalp.

They shaved my head!

"I'm sorry," Brooklyn said, touching Simone gently on the fore-arm. "I had to ask about the drugs thing. Even though I pretty much know she's clean."

Every single supposed sighting of Taylor out partying had proved bogus after Brooklyn investigated. Twitter might be a great tool for social media marketers, Photoshop fiends, and for feuding with idiots, but Brooklyn found it a total failure as a credible news source.

"That's why I came to you," Simone said. "You've been nothing but fair to Taylor—even when everyone else is writing crap that isn't true."

"Thanks, but first I need the guest list for the party."

"Of course. It was only like twenty people, maybe thirty. It was super small. I just sent out texts to everyone."

"Okay, and did you take any pictures?"

"Yeah, but only on my cell. We made every guest check cells at the front door. We didn't want any pictures leaking out. It was a private party. Just kids. No adults. No media and stuff."

"That didn't really work out very well," Brooklyn joked.

Simone giggled.

"We are going to find her—I promise." Brooklyn set her phone down in her lap. "But I have to ask. Simone, why haven't you gone to the police yet?"

Simone hugged her arms around herself and started rocking slowly back and forth. She stared into the park beside the stadium where Holden was walking away.

"I can't," she said. "I'm afraid of what they might to do me."

"They?"

"The cops."

"Why?"

"I could go to jail."

"Simone, they can't put you in jail for reporting someone missing. If there's anything I need to know, please tell me now." Brooklyn tilted her head. "If you don't trust me, you have every right to get up and leave and go find someone else. As much as I want to make sure we find Taylor, I can't waste my time on this if you aren't going to entirely trust me."

Simone sat back down and pushed her sleeves down to cover her hands. "You're right. The truth is that I really don't think those guys with the guns were cops."

"Then who were they?"

"I don't know for sure, but I sort of think they were working with this guy I invited."

"A friend of Taylor's?"

"Not really, just this random cute guy. He claimed he was an agent's assistant, and he had been trying to meet Taylor for the last few weeks. He was literally begging me for an invite to her birthday party."

"And why did you give it to him?"

Simone exhaled. "Okay, I realize this is going to make me look really bad, and I want to say that I feel totally guilty for doing this, but the reason I invited him was because A) He was hot and B) He promised me he would bring drugs—but not for Taylor, I swear. Just for the rest of us. And he did bring drugs. A lot of them."

"Like?"

"Molly, Ecstasy, maybe a little coke, too."

"Is that all?"

"Well . . ." Simone looked away. "Some Adderall and Oxy."

Brooklyn had never seen a person do drugs in real life. She stopped typing. "A walking Walgreens!"

Simone hung her head. "I know, I know. And you're probably thinking I'm a totally horrible human being. There was a whole stash of drugs inside the house when those cops, or whoever they were, came and shut down the party."

"So this guy, this drug dealer dude or whatever, came to the party, and you had a pharmacy of drugs on you, and that's why you ran?"

"Pretty much. Totally panicked. And by the time I realized what was happening, the guys with the guns had dragged Taylor outside through the gate. I didn't know who to turn to afterward. Except you." Simone sighed. "Brooklyn, this is literally the entire story. Swear."

"But why do you think these guys only wanted Taylor?"

"To kidnap her? Hold her for ransom?" Simone asked. "She was the only celeb. I mean, Evan was invited, but he didn't come, and there weren't any other celeb types there. I don't know. Why else would they take her away except maybe for money?"

"If it's for a ransom, it's already been two days and they haven't made any demands. That makes me think this might be about more than money."

Simone crunched her eyes. "You know, most sixteen-year-old girls I meet aren't anything like you."

"Blame my parents," Brooklyn answered. "They let me watch way too much TV as a kid. My friends call me 'G-ma' for being able to remember every plot line from shows like *Law & Order* and *CSI*. My parents always thought I would end up wanting to be a cop or a lawyer or something. But I picked journalism. That way I still get to solve mysteries, but without the ulcers. Or the guns."

"What do your parents do?"

"Mom's a lawyer. But not like one of those rich lawyers. She's a public defender."

"So she defends criminals?"

"*Alleged* criminals."

"Okay." Simone fashioned air quotes. "Alleged."

"She loves it, even though she has to work like fifteen hours a day. And my dad, he was a cop. Twenty-two years on the Twin Oaks Police force."

"A cop?" Simone's eyes widened. "You're not going to tell *him* about me, are you?"

"I won't be telling him anything."

"You promise? Because that would be really bad. The cops can't know all that stuff about the drugs."

"I definitely won't be telling my dad anything."

"Why?"

"Because he's dead."

Simone's mouth dropped open.

Brooklyn rubbed Simone's shoulder and got to her feet. "It's okay. This bench is killing me, by the way. Let's go for a walk."

They stepped off the bleachers and walked over to the Coffee Cartel in a strip mall across the street from campus.

As Brooklyn scrolled through Simone's cell phone pics, Simone fished inside her purse.

"You smoke?" Simone asked. "'Cuz I'm all out."

"Do you run across the 101 at rush hour?" Brooklyn asked.

"Hell no. I'm not stupid!"

"Exactly my point. You're *not* stupid. You don't want to die! So why do you smoke? Smoking is my least favorite thing that humans do—besides making bad TV shows, bullying vulnerable people, and starting pointless wars."

"Okay, okay, fine." Simone tapped her coffee cup on the table and bit the nail of her pinkie finger. "I can't disagree with you. But I still really need a smoke."

"Why do so many people in Hollywood smoke, anyway?"

"Good question." Simone pressed her lips together. "I think it starts off as something you do when you're bored at parties. And then it becomes something you do instead of eating. By the time you've gotten that far into it, it's really hard to stop. You're hooked, addicted. I know this from personal experience. It sucks."

"Finally! An honest answer from you!"

"Hey, I've been honest," Simone said with a laugh. "Okay, maybe not at first I wasn't."

"To say the least."

Brooklyn knew a Hollywood girl like Simone would never be friends with someone like her. But she was enjoying hanging out with her, despite the circumstances.

"I'm glad you came to me," Brooklyn said. "I won't disappoint you, and I won't betray your trust. You have my word."

"I know you won't. It's just that being an assistant to someone as famous as Taylor Prince, you learn pretty quickly that you can't trust everyone, so you end up not trusting anyone at all."

"I get it. My dad used to always say, 'Even if your mother says she loves you, check your sources.'"

"About that." Simone cleared her throat twice. "I'm really sorry about your dad. How old were you when he died?"

"Twelve."

"Wow, that's super recent. I can't imagine. My parents drive me nuts, but I know I am lucky to have both of them alive. That is just so harsh."

"Yeah, it was, and it still is. That's life, I guess."

Brooklyn didn't normally open up so easily to strangers, but having seen Simone in so many photos over the last couple years and following her movements with Taylor on Instagram, she seemed familiar, almost like a friend.

Still, Brooklyn didn't tell Simone how she spent six months in a near-catatonic state after her father's death. She didn't reveal that she could barely get off the couch, where she would spend days watching TV and movies and napping and crying. And then crying some more.

During her couch potato period, she rented the movie *Girl on the Verge*, starring Taylor Prince. Brooklyn had a big-time girl crush, her first ever, and she decided that her purpose in life was to obsessively track every move of Taylor Prince and then share the news with other fans on a website. Starting *DeadlineDiaries.com* knocked Brooklyn out of her father-grieving funk while also making her realize she wanted to be an entertainment journalist.

But per her lawyerly usual self, Brooklyn's mother pointed out the holes in her career choice.

"Brooklyn, real journalists can't just write about what they want when they want," her mother lectured. "They get assigned stories and are given actual deadlines. You can't even get your math homework handed in on time."

The next day Brooklyn borrowed her mom's credit card and plunked down $12.99 to register "DeadlineDiaries.com," and some four years later, Brooklyn had met self-imposed deadlines every day and expanded her coverage to include all young celebrities, not just Taylor Prince.

Brooklyn swiped her way through a few dozen shots on Simone's phone. Most were of random chicks and dudes posing with girls in tiny dresses. Taylor looked gorgeous in all the pics, wearing bright-red lipstick that matched her red heels.

"So which one of these guys is the drug guy?" Brooklyn asked.

Simone enlarged a pic of Taylor swinging her arm around a good-looking guy with short dark hair. "That's him."

"You weren't kidding." Brooklyn leaned in closer to the picture. "He's actually *really* hot. What's his name?"

"I don't know. I met him at a club and he gave me his number. He called himself 'B.'"

"I guess when you're that hot, a name becomes pretty unimportant."

"Sad but true."

"I'm going to need his name," Brooklyn said. "If he doesn't know where Taylor is, he might know someone who does. Now that we have a picture, Holden can work his magic. I'm gonna text him."

"And he definitely won't know I'm the source, right?"

"He won't. But be very careful. I don't want to freak you out, but you're the closest person to Taylor and so they might still be looking for you."

Simone's face went white. She looked out the window at the cars behind them in the parking lot. Range Rover with tinted windows. Random guy sitting alone in a Honda. Soccer mom checking her teeth in the rearview mirror of a minivan.

Brooklyn lowered the brim of her baseball cap to her eyebrows and scanned the perimeter of the strip mall lot. "At this point, until we know where Taylor is and who took her, we have to assume anything is possible."

Sweaty forehead. Dry mouth. Pounding heart.

The air labored in and out of Taylor's lungs. She wheezed, trying desperately to reverse the sudden panic attack that had come on after she realized she was locked inside the room.

The last time Taylor had a full-on episode was that horrible day she came home from school in third grade and learned that her dad had died.

Now Taylor felt like she was the one dying.

Breathe in . . . and out, she repeated over and over and over, just as her yoga instructor had taught her. The yoga instructor Simone had introduced her to. The yoga instructor who, like everyone else in her life that mattered most, was now outside the walls that contained her.

In the silence of her locked room, she could hear the sound of dogs barking outside. They'd growl and bark, then stop. Then bark again in a wolflike shrill. Coyotes howled back from up in the cactus-dotted hills.

A sharp pain shot up Taylor's right ankle. It throbbed like last summer when she stepped on a stingray at Malibu cove.

She bent over and reached for her foot, and she saw something etched on the back of the ankle. Taylor blinked her eyes until the black marking came into focus:

$$\frac{\infty}{2}$$

The characters were no bigger than those on a keyboard. She pressed her thumb against them and started rubbing, hoping they were just the product of an erasable marker. But it only made her soft skin grow more irritated. She licked her thumb and rubbed more.

Taylor leaped from the bed and once again pounded on the metal door, screaming for help. But no one came. She collapsed to the floor.

Her gorgeous long hair had defined her beauty, and now she lay bald and crying on the cold tile in a fetal position, praying for her nightmare to end.

Brooklyn counted. Four final sips of her iced tea. Simone also finished off her drink. On their way out Brooklyn counted four stirring straws in the bin next to the sugar jar.

She pressed her thumb into her palm, leaving four fingers stretched out.

Brooklyn scanned the parked cars as she and Simone snaked their way through. Every fourth step, Brooklyn scratched her nose for good luck, and when they got to Simone's black BMW sedan, she jumped shotgun.

"Act normal," Brooklyn said, looking in the side mirror as Simone backed out. "At that stop sign, hang a left—and don't look back."

"Anyone behind us?" Simone glanced into the rearview mirror.

"Just keep driving. Turn here, at the light."

Brooklyn spotted a car that had been about 100 yards behind them on El Camino also turn right. "I don't like the looks of that silver car."

One of Brooklyn's fondest childhood memories was when she and her dad played "the tail game," where they would pretend to be followed by a bad guy while driving around town and make several seemingly nonsensical turns that amounted to a giant circle. Her dad called the game "SD," short for "Surveillance Detection."

But this time the SD routine didn't come with the same fun. This was not a game.

"Hang another right—up here." Brooklyn pointed at the rapidly approaching residential side street off the boulevard. Simone hit the brakes hard and made a hasty turn onto the street.

Clenching her teeth, Brooklyn checked the mirror. She counted to four for good luck. A long four. The silver car sped by the turn and kept straight on the boulevard.

Brooklyn released the air from her lungs. "Phew—false alarm."

"Jesus, Brooklyn!" Simone pounded the dashboard. "You scared the crap out of me!"

"Hey, I'd rather be extra paranoid than extra dead."

Simone nodded. "Okay, but now what?"

"I need to do some digging. So just drop me off at home. I'll text you later tonight."

As directed, Simone pulled up in front of the brown stucco ranch house at the end of Sierra Drive.

"I guess it's true what they say about redheads," Simone said.

Brooklyn arched her eyebrows. "That we are the human embodiment of beastly sexual desire, as well as the root of all evil?"

"No." Simone laughed. "That you're intense."

"Yeah, we are." Brooklyn tapped the toe of her right foot four times on the floor mat, then opened the passenger door. "But mostly just when things don't go our way."

"Fifty-one fifty," the short man said deliberately. "You're on a 5150 Hold of the California Welfare and Institutions Code."

Stitched in green cursive script on the left side of the man's white smock was "Helper George." Taylor studied his black hair, so dark it looked as if it was painted over with shoe polish. His beady eyes showed no wrinkles around them, even when he blinked. His forehead had the smoothness of a freshly Zambonied sheet of ice.

"I don't get it," Taylor said, confused.

"It's simply a safety precaution." He smiled. "You need not worry. Any person deemed by a mental health professional to be a danger to themselves or others can be held—against their will—in a psychiatric lockup for up to seventy-two hours."

"So you're saying I'm crazy."

"Not exactly. That's why you are being evaluated in our care. We are trying to figure out, clinically, the extent of your issues."

"But what would make you think I'm nuts? I'm probably the most normal person I know. I am so normal I am boring. Despite what you might read on the blogs."

George opened the manila folder he'd been clutching and read from the piece of paper on top. "According to our admission report, you locked yourself in the bathroom of your house on Saturday and threatened to kill yourself if anyone tried to come in. Does that jog your memory at all, Ms. Prince?"

"No. Not at all."

"We have sworn statements from several eyewitnesses, including a Simone Witten."

"That's my assistant." Taylor looked down at the "Helper" on George's coat and backed up. "Who do you help, by the way?"

"You."

"Besides me."

"The doctor."

"Which doctor?"

"You'll be meeting him shortly. Like I said, your assistant told investigators that you had been under the influence of drugs and had been threatening to kill yourself several times that night. According to her statement, you shaved off all your hair with a razor—and then threatened to cut your wrists."

"Sir, I can promise you that Simone would never say anything like that. She knows me better than anyone else, and that's just not true. I love life. I love my hair. This is totally insane—"

"Are you sure all this is not true or do you just not remember?" George asked in a condescending tone that made her want to hurt him. "There's a big difference."

Taylor looked beyond George out the window at the palm grove and lush green lawn. "That's a bullshit trick question."

"All I'm saying, Ms. Prince, is that it's not uncommon for someone who experienced a psychotic episode to have no memory of it. It's the brain's way of protecting itself from incurring even more trauma."

Maybe I am crazy. Maybe I did shave my head. But why?

"We've contacted your mother," George continued. "She, of course, is quite concerned, and will be making her way here to see you very soon. She has contacted everyone on your team as well. She realizes you are under excellent care."

"I want to talk to her," Taylor said. "I have that right."

"Ms. Prince, you don't." He shrugged. "At least not until your seventy-two hour hold has expired. Our focus at the moment is on diagnostics and getting you healthy while we complete our investigation."

"So how long have I been locked up here?"

George glanced at his watch. "A little over fifty-five hours."

So she had just a little over a day to convince them she wasn't crazy. It was a role—that of a sane, well-adjusted, not-crazy sixteen-year-old girl—that she was convinced she could pull off. Though if she did threaten to kill herself, and if she did, in fact, repress that memory, she could be a total whack job. But the last thing she wanted to do was let on that she had any doubts.

Act sane.

"So where am I exactly?" she asked.

"The Kensington Center for Wellness and Rejuvenation. We are the state's most respected center for the treatment of psychiatric and addiction-related issues for teens. If you haven't heard of our program, I'm sure you're familiar with some of our members." George rattled off a who's who of young celebrities who have been treated there over the last few years—Brianna Jean, Savannah Ramirez, Remy Sky, just to name a few.

"Needless to say, you're in excellent hands here with us. You may say we specialize in catering to the unique needs of high-profile young people such as yourself."

Act normal.

She flashed him her ankle marking. "Can you at least explain this?"

"Your member ID."

"A tattoo? Is this really necessary?"

"That's the infinity symbol," George said. "Kensington offers its members a permanent solution, and lifelong membership."

"What's the number two all about?"

"That's your member number."

"What about all the others you mentioned?"

"They were patients. Not *members*."

Taylor sighed. "Just tell me when I can leave."

George placed his hand gently on her shoulder. "First you must get pure. It's been said that a pure soul is like a fine pearl. When a pearl is hidden in its shell, no one even thinks of admiring it. But if you bring it out of its shell, the pearl will shine and attract all eyes." His grin pinched upward. "Kensington will help you shine again."

Knock, knock.

Brooklyn groaned.

Knock, knock, knock.

Brooklyn shouted, "ONE MORE, PLEASE!"

She had told her mom at least a thousand times that it was bad luck for her to answer after just three knocks. She needed four.

Knock, knock, knock . . . KNOCK.

"Come in!"

The door opened with her mother holding two bags of groceries, a healthy head of lettuce billowing from the top of one.

"How may I help you, Mrs. Brant?" Brooklyn said.

"Got you some Whole Foods," her mom said. "Wanna come and join me for a salad? I've got quinoa. Brain food."

"I'd love to, but I'm working on a story. I'm real busy. Plus, I just had a sandwich."

Her mom put the grocery bags down and Brooklyn could hear the sound of glass bottles clanking against each other. *Great, drink more wine to drown your sorrows.*

Mrs. Brant leaned in for a peek. "What's the story?"

"Just a casting item about the next season of *Obsessed.* They're adding a hot new guy to play Nina's lab partner. No biggie, but I have to post it before I get scooped."

"All right then."

"What's the problem?"

"Nothing, except that I'd like to spend some quality time with you before summer break ends next month and our schedules get even more crazy. Maybe you should take a break from the blog for a few hours, have some dinner. Come watch *Law & Order* with me like the old days."

Here we go again.

"You know, just lighten your load a little," her mom continued. "Relax. Get some sun. Make new friends other than that Tamara."

"Mom . . ."

"And whatever happened to that soccer boy, Andy Bowen?"

"Mom."

"He asked you to the junior prom, right?"

"All brawn, no brains."

"Well, I thought he was pretty sweet and handsome."

"Try *blandsome*."

"My point is that you've closed yourself off."

Brooklyn turned her focus back to her computer. "This is the point in our conversation where I go, 'Okay, thanks for caring,' and then go back to blogging because I'm on a deadline, and you respect my work ethic and are simply happy that I'm not hanging out at a party getting wasted or pregnant or something."

"Brookie, I'm not asking you to stop blogging, just to—"

"Take a break." Brooklyn finished her sentence. "Because I'm too young to be working all the time. Because ever since Dad died I've been too serious and don't have enough fun. Because you're worried that I have socially withdrawn and don't have enough friends. Because Dad would want me to have more balance in my life. Trust me, I know the speech."

Her mother groaned. "Okaaay, Brookie Cookie. Whatever you say."

She firmed her grip on the grocery bags and walked down the hall.

"Love you, Mom!"

Brooklyn wasn't lying about working on a story. In fact, she did just break the casting news about Lance Wilder joining *Obsessed* next season, which she had confirmed with the head writer of the show, a great source she had found last year after stalking him on Twitter and becoming friends via DM.

Brooklyn had seen all twenty-four episodes of *Obsessed*, for which she could recite most of the exact plots. Because of her DM relationship with the head writer, she broke a lot of stories about the show. Yet network spokespeople rarely officially confirmed these stories to her, and instead hand-delivered exclusives to the trades or other mainstream websites and publications.

Earlier, Simone had emailed Brooklyn the names of the thirteen people invited to the party, minus the name of the hot guy. Everyone on the guest list except for Pretty Boy was a close friend of Taylor's. Not one of them was suspicious in any way.

While Simone didn't have his name, she did have a cell number she had been texting.

Brooklyn had gotten pretty good at using background databases to locate people, especially with her secret cyber-weapon of her dad's old FaceFinder program. He had used it for his detective investigations, and some four years after his death, it still had not been shut off. Using his password and username, she could input a cell phone number, and after auto-searching hundreds of data sources, the program almost always spit back an address or a name attached to it. *Almost* always.

The number Simone had for the mystery guy was not connected to any individual, which usually meant that it was either a temporary phone or a phone owned by a company. That meant she would have to assign this challenge to her crack research "staff."

> hey Holdenboo . . . I'm stuck. Need ur help tracking a #

> send it over. I'll see what I can do!

No blinking. From what Taylor observed, Lily had a set of wide blue eyes that rarely—if ever—closed. They. Just. Stared. Like creepy doll eyes.

"You'll remember everything we discuss in this Delete Session," Lily said. She sat across from Taylor, who was in a black leather reclining chair that reminded her of the dentist.

"A *what* kind of session?" Taylor replied.

"Delete Session, a healing therapy created by Dr. Kensington. It simply is the best method for overcoming traumas and helping you get past your addictions. You'll see. It worked for me and all the other helpers. The key to discovering your inner innocent child is the key to unlocking eternal happiness."

Taylor guessed Lily was somewhere in her forties. Her middle-aged skin stretched back toward her ears like a creaseless latex mask, failing miserably at making her look twenty years younger but succeeding in making her look like a humanoid.

"You have the power to clear out any blockages in your mind that may be holding your life back—be it in your career, love life, your health," Lily continued. "You can trust me, Taylor. Do you?"

"Yes," Taylor lied. "I trust you."

"Okay, then I can help you. First, close your eyes. And now, whenever I say the word 'delete' in a therapy session, you will be able to remove it from memory. It will no longer have any power over you. That is the key to the Program."

"What's the Program?"

"Helper George hasn't told you?"

"He did meet with me earlier this morning. But he didn't mention any specific program."

"And what about Dr. Kensington?"

"Who?"

Lily tapped more notes into her tablet, a few seconds later adding, "I apologize for any confusion. But it's not my place to discuss the Program. I'm only a Helper."

"Then if you're such a *helper*, you should help me understand."

"The doctor can. It's not my place."

"Which doctor?"

"Again, I'm sorry. I can't. As you will learn, Dr. Kensington believes there are two types of people in the world: Helpers and Hurters. It's important to know your role in this binary system. That's how you can be most effective in helping anyone."

Taylor looked around the windowless evaluation room. Every wall was painted sky blue except the one to her right, which was a floor-to-ceiling mirror. She noticed the dark circles under her eyes and her ghostly skin tone in the reflection.

"Now if you would just close your eyes we can get started on the Work," Lily said.

"Okay, let's do this."

"Very good. So let's begin with you recalling an incident in your life that has had a negative impact on you. Any one will do."

Taylor wanted to answer "being locked up in this 'wellness' center in the desert by a bunch of lunatics." Instead she said, "I remember not getting picked for the lead in *Annie*."

"When was this incident?" Lily asked.

"Fifth grade, I think."

"How did it make you feel?"

"Mad."

"Why?"

"Because I deserved to get the lead. I was better than Ally O'Hara."

"Why does it still bother you so much?"

"Because I believe in fairness, not in playing favorites. And I can't stand it when something is done that isn't fair. It demoralizes you."

"You do understand that life isn't fair sometimes?"

"Of course, I do."

Lily locked eyes with Taylor. "Then you must *delete*."

Taylor let out a rush of air and stared back at her stiff "helper," who hadn't moved from her cross-legged position. "Lily, I'm really sorry, but I don't think you need to lecture me about life not being fair. I don't see how that has anything to do with me proving that I am not a harm to myself or to others, which is supposedly the reason I am here."

Lily stared back, stone-faced and emotionless. "Okay, let's continue. Please, close your eyes again. And remember that when I say 'delete' you will wipe whatever we've been talking about from your memory."

Taylor glared at her. "Fine." She pinched her eyes shut.

"Now, do you think you will ever be able to think about that incident and not grow upset or agitated?"

"I'm not upset or agitated by that incident." Taylor fought hard to keep her eyes closed. "It just bothers me that it was blatantly unfair. I'm only upset that you are trying to make some big deal out of this, especially when the bigger deal is that you people are trying to make me feel like I'm out of my mind when, clearly, I am not."

"Taylor, I am merely the Helper, and part of the helping process is to identify and delete negative influences that may have led you here. That is my only goal. I have no intention of upsetting you any more than you already are."

Taylor realized she probably had already said too much. "You're right. I'm sorry. I do trust you."

"Okay, good. Now close your eyes."

She closed them again, though under silent protest.

"Okay," Lily said, "now when I snap my fingers, I will say

'delete,' and you will visualize that memory of not getting the lead role in the play disappearing from your brain's desktop and being put in the trash."

Lily snapped her fingers and said with all the personality of a computerized GPS voice, "Delete."

The two of them sat silently for several seconds, until Lily said, "Now you may open your eyes. Do you feel refreshed?"

"Totally!" Taylor opened her eyes, flashed her multimillion-dollar smile, and stretched her arms over her head. She yawned. "Totally rejuvenated."

"A crack?" Brooklyn's mom picked her daughter's phone off the bedroom floor. "A tiny little crack?"

She sat on the edge of Brooklyn's bed and examined the missing piece of glass in the upper right corner of the screen. "Is this why you're having a meltdown?"

Brooklyn could smell the fruity odor of chardonnay on her mother's breath, a scent that had become all too familiar since her mom was widowed. Brooklyn buried her face in her pillow and growled.

"Honey, it's just a phone," her mother said, not quite slurring but not sounding quite sober, either. She rubbed her daughter's back as Brooklyn used the white pillowcase as a Kleenex. "I'm sorry, but I really don't understand what the big deal is."

No one did. No one could understand her inner torment. No one realized how much she needed all four corners of her phone screen to be perfectly intact. She couldn't tell her mom this. It would just set into motion awkward conversations and weekly therapy sessions in which the shrink would remind her how unnecessary her counting-to-four routine was.

"We can go to the store in the morning and get a replacement." Her mom hit the Power button and the phone popped alive. "Hey, look, it still works! See, there's nothing to worry about. Plus, Brookie, there are bigger problems in the world than your phone."

"I'm okay," Brooklyn mumbled. "I just dropped it."

"Are you sure you are okay? It's been quite a while since I've seen you like this."

Two years ago the OCD diagnosed by her therapist got so bad that Brooklyn had to drop out of school for three months and be home-schooled—and she had to sit on Dr. Kramer's couch three days a week talking about the same thing over and over. She knew her mom was purposely *not* mentioning that episode, but it was clearly her motherly fear.

"I'm seriously okay, just a little hormonal."

Her mom sat down on the edge of the bed and rubbed circles between Brooklyn's shoulder blades. "I think this blog might be causing you too much stress. Maybe getting out and being more social would help things. Maybe you could even get a real job."

"My blog is a real job. I just don't make money."

"Real jobs pay you real money, my dear."

"I'd rather kill myself than work at Jamba Juice."

"Honey, don't talk like that."

"Not literally, Mom. My blog is what keeps me sane, makes me feel alive. And I'm making progress on the profit side."

In the last two years, the number of unique monthly visitors to *DeadlineDiaries.com* had gone from zero to about half a million. And that was with only updating her site four days a week. Now the site was being linked to by major entertainment news sites on a regular basis. Revenue sharing from blogger ads brought in enough to pay for photos and monthly storage and hosting fees. But *Deadline Diaries* was not yet a money-making enterprise. Not even close.

Holden had presented Brooklyn with some ideas for ways to "monetize" page views—more videos, more photo slide shows, a more aggressive social media presence (including actually posting pictures of herself), investing in a Search Engine Optimization consultant. But Brooklyn had always resisted. If the only thing her blog did was disseminate truth and quality content, all the while bolstering her high school resume, that would be enough for her.

Until now.

Now Brooklyn wanted to break a story that would elevate her above the major sites, even *STARSTALK*. If she could unravel the story behind Taylor's disappearance, if she indeed had gone missing and not been shipped to rehab like so many celebs before her, then Brooklyn might have found her Holy Grail. But she knew that only old-fashioned journalism could achieve this goal.

After her mom walked out of the room, Brooklyn crawled out of bed and opened her laptop.

Bzzzzz.

Holden.

No luck. that # is untraceable. Tried. ☹

blah Ok. Thanks

That Pulitzer Prize would have to wait.

No TV.

No computer.

No phone.

No Simone.

Taylor imagined that life inside Kensington roughly resembled life in the 1800s—no fun in any way, shape, or form.

That is, except for the food and the exercise program. Taylor did a Bikram yoga session with helper Lily in the super-heated fitness room. And she had been fed like a natural foods princess. Gluten-free toast with almond butter for breakfast. Albacore sashimi and miso soup for lunch. Free-range chicken and jasmine brown rice for dinner. The nurse—the same one who delivered the rehab news—also delivered the meals to her room, calling them the "detox diet." As frighteningly isolated as Taylor was, she saw a silver lining in knowing that at least she wouldn't be getting fat.

The nurse entered her room, this time accompanied by George. She pushed a wheeled cart, from which dangled a clear plastic bag filled with fluid. A narrow plastic tube about three feet long swung from the bottom of the bag.

"According to our research here at Kensington, our organ functions' decline is due in large part to our body's inability to absorb the necessary levels of nutrients as we age. Intravenous entry is the most efficient way of getting high-dose nutrients into your blood stream. It boosts your immune system, reduces inflammation, increases your energy levels. This weekly IV nutrient therapy is essential to the Program and will commence today," George said.

The nurse positioned the IV pole beside Taylor's left arm

and pulled a five-inch-long needle from her pocket. "Why not just let me swallow vitamins?" Taylor asked.

"Oral ingestion has its limits and complications," George replied. "Not only will the nutrients be more quickly absorbed this way, but at this high dosage you can have gastrointestinal issues such as bowel blockages and the like."

"Lovely," Taylor said.

The nurse straightened Taylor's arm flat on the bed and swabbed the area around her arm bend with an alcohol wipe. She tied a rubber band around Taylor's bicep and pressed her thumb onto the surface above a vein. Then she brought the catheter needle to the skin and poked through. Taylor winced. The nurse connected the IV tube to the catheter and opened the valve, letting the clear fluid drip into her arm.

George held up his phone in camera position. "Give me a thumbs-up!" he said.

Taylor flashed a faux smile and a set of cheesy thumb pistols. George snapped a photo. "We document everything," he explained.

"You said I need to do this weekly?" Taylor asked.

"That's correct."

"But if I got here early Sunday, then my 5150 hold should expire right about now. Or at least very soon."

Which meant, she hoped, that Kensington could no longer legally hold her against her will. She had certainly proven she was not a threat to herself or to others, and, in fact, was starting to feel downright pure and rejuvenated!

"Of course, yes," George said. "But it's all pending the results of your intake evaluation."

Taylor had already fantasized about what she would do immediately upon her release. She would call her mom and explain everything so she wouldn't worry. Then she would call Simone, have her come pick her up, go home and pack, and then head off to Mexico for that weeklong sixteenth birthday vacation they had been planning for the last two months.

The room door buzzed open and in walked one of the three steroidal-looking security guards Taylor had seen roaming the halls and grounds of the clinic over the last day.

"Good afternoon, Ms. Prince," said the guard.

"Greetings!" she replied with a sunny smile.

The guard handed George a printout, and George read it intently.

"We have some good news and we have some bad news," George said, standing just in front of the security guard at the foot of her bed.

Taylor swallowed what little saliva was left in her mouth.

"The good news is that your family and your professional management team—including your agent, publicist, and manager—have been made aware of your personal situation. And they are one hundred percent supportive of you and send their love." He glanced down at the paper on his clipboard. "As for the bad news . . ."

Taylor propped herself straight up with her hands on the mattress.

"We have the results of your toxicology test."

Swim class (aka an hour of hell she was only withstanding to appease her mother). Since swim class was co-ed, Brooklyn took solace in having Holden participate in her misery, not to mention slather sunscreen all over her skin in preparation. You know, as any "friend" might.

But then her walk home with Holden became anything but heartening.

"No way." Brooklyn's eyes stayed glued to her phone. "No way."

"What?" Holden asked.

"No freaking way. Holy crap. Oh my god. I can't believe—"

Brooklyn kicked off her flip-flops and clutched them tightly in one hand. Taking off down the sidewalk, Brooklyn was ten yards ahead of Holden before he even noticed.

"Where are you going?" he shouted.

"Home!" she shouted back without stopping. "Check out *STARSTALK*!"

As much as Brooklyn despised *STARSTALK*'s "checkbook" journalism—not to mention their atrocious track record of misinformation and fake stories—they could not be ignored. Especially with their current headline:

TAYLOR PRINCE REHAB SHOCKER: SEX, DRUGS, AND SUICIDE?!?! CLICK **HERE** FOR THE EXCLUSIVE PIC!!!

At home, a photo of Taylor filled Brooklyn's computer screen, her head shaved to the point of near baldness, crying. Underneath the photo was a block of text:

Sources exclusively reveal to STARSTALK that teen actress Taylor Prince has been holed up in a California rehab facility for the last three days following a drug-filled night of partying that ended with the once-revered star shaving her head and threatening to kill herself. Only STARSTALK can report that Prince is now being treated at an undisclosed addiction treatment center. Calls to Prince's rep went unanswered, but when contacted by STARSTALK via phone in Arizona, Prince's mother replied, "We are praying for our daughter. We have no further comment."

As STARSTALK has reported exclusively many times in recent months, Prince has been secretly struggling with an addiction to opiate painkillers and other drugs, a habit enabled by her long-time assistant and friend, Simone Witten. Says a source: "The plan right now is to cut out all the bad people in Taylor's life, get her clean and back to the world-class talent she was before her slide."

STARSTALK will remain on top of the story and will update with the latest developments.

Not only did Brooklyn feel betrayed by Simone, now she felt completely gullible, like an amateurish high school blogger rather than the kind of journalist she actually was.

She had been dumb enough to believe Simone's tall tale. Obviously, anyone who would invite a drug dealer to her friend's birthday party could not to be trusted. She knew sources with personal agendas often fed journalists misinformation to help their own selfish cause or interest, but fabricating an entire tale of kidnapping really took the cake!

She texted Simone.

> thanks for wasting my time, LIAR. Plz lose
> my #

Brooklyn paused. Feeling guilty, she added:

> but may God bless you . . . you need it.

Brooklyn was reading and re-reading the *STARSTALK* story, analyzing it for any clues as to who their sources might be, when Holden walked into her bedroom.

"Knocking go out of style?" Brooklyn asked.

"Sorry," Holden said. "But what the heck's going on?"

"*This* is going on." Brooklyn pointed at her laptop.

Holden leaned in. "So this was the story you had me helping you with?"

"Yeah, well, sort of. That girl at the track was telling me a different version of the story. Much different."

"So Simone Witten was that source?"

"Usually I'd never reveal a source, but since she is looking like a totally bogus, lying sack of crap, I don't mind telling you that, yes, she is the idiot-liar source of mine."

Holden put his hands on his hips. "But how often would you estimate that *STARSTALK* is right?"

"I don't know. Maybe half the time. If that."

"So couldn't their story also have a fifty percent chance of being *wrong*?"

"Maybe."

"And what was your dad's saying about most of the cases he investigated?"

"That there are always three sides to every story," Brooklyn said. "The accuser's story, the accused's story, and then the truth."

"So maybe the truth is somewhere in between the *STARSTALK* report and Simone's. I mean, why would Simone totally make up everything like that?"

"It's obvious. Simone could have been trying to cover her own butt because she knew all the dirt on her was about to come out. Think about it. It's your basic slick PR damage control. Get your side of the story out first since that usually becomes the storyline people are more likely to believe."

"Fine, maybe Simone is lying," Holden replied. "But what if she is right and *STARSTALK* is wrong?"

"Then I just blew it." She sighed.

"Why?"

"Because I just told Simone to lose my number."

"The results," George announced from Taylor's bedside. "I have them here."

The nurse removed the catheter from Taylor's arm, soaking up a dribble of blood and covering the wound with a cotton ball and single strip of white medical tape.

A pair of goateed security guards also stood in Taylor's room. George handed Taylor a copy of her toxicology report: A bullet-pointed list of all the substances for which she had apparently tested positive—heroin, cocaine, benzodiazepines, and amphetamines. As she read the report, George said, "Your *temporary* seventy-two-hour involuntary hold has been officially extended for another fourteen days."

In other words, she was stuck for two more weeks inside an antiseptic land of creepy liars. "I've never done a drug in my life," Taylor said.

Taylor flung the papers in the air and flew from her bed and across the floor toward the man. Clenching her right fist into a tight ball, Taylor twisted her body to the left and then snapped it to the right, the backside of her balled-up hand going smack into George's nose. Blood gushed from George's nostrils, as well as from Taylor's left arm where the IV puncture hadn't yet clotted.

The security goons tackled Taylor, and with one holding her by the feet and the other by her arms, they carried her thrashing body down the hall. The more she squirmed, the harder they squeezed.

"Let me go!"

When they reached the end of the hall, a steel door unlocked with a buzz. The men pushed the door open and dropped Taylor on the tile floor in a windowless room smaller than her mansion's walk-in closet. All four walls were lined with thick padding. The men left, slamming the door shut behind them.

She sat up, pressed her back against the wall, and buried her face in her hands. If she had any hair left, she certainly would have pulled it out. Instead, she just howled and moaned and wept until her eyes dried out.

When the door opened at least an hour later, Taylor, now in the fetal position, didn't even bother to get up.

Just kill me.

In walked an elf of a man with a shade of blond hair that could never have occurred naturally. He was overly tan with a smooth-shaven face and wore a white button-down shirt, white seersucker pants, and a canary sport coat with a green silk handkerchief tucked in the chest pocket that made him look like an Easter egg come to life.

"Congratulations, Ms. Prince." He spoke precisely and in a high-pitched voice more boy than man. Beaming, he handed her a bottle of coconut water.

Taylor pressed herself to standing, took the water and gulped from it.

"You're the first female patient to receive the White Room treatment," he said. "That's quite an achievement, though a dubious one at that."

Taylor guzzled the rest of the bottle.

"Now that you've calmed down, let's go get some fresh air, eh? Let's say we go for a little stroll across the courtyard to my place."

Taylor slowly walked toward him, dragging her slippers along the white tile.

As he opened the door, Taylor asked, "Where are Tweedle-dee and Tweedledum?"

The man chuckled. "Oh yes, they're right outside your door. I left them out there because I'm not afraid of you. In fact, there is no bigger fan of Taylor Prince than myself. And I have been a big fan for quite some time. I'm Dr. Peter Kensington."

Dr. Kensington reached out his hand, and it felt smooth to the touch, as if from a lifetime of moisturizering. "Call me Peter."

The doctor clutched two straw hats. He handed the wide-brimmed, floppier one to Taylor, and placed the smaller men's style hat on his own head. The black chinstrap dangling below his angular chin made him look like a little boy on a pony ride.

Taylor followed the doctor into the hallway and past her 200-pound-plus tacklers.

Losers.

The doctor, whom she stood over by at least two inches, strolled with arrogant ease through the automatic sliding glass front door. He pulled a pair of thick-framed sunglasses from his pants pocket. He held a rigid posture, chin up and chest out, like a lord in his manor. A Napoleon complex, Taylor diagnosed.

The palm-lined stone pathway was surrounded by a lawn that extended a hundred yards on both sides to a wall circling the property. "Five hundred acres," Dr. Kensington boasted. "I bought this land a long time ago, back in the nineties. It used to be a Cabazon tribal burial ground."

Taylor squinted in the harsh sunlight. A pack of four German shepherds darted across the lawn at full speed in her direction. "*Nein, nein!*" Peter held his right arm high above his head. "*Nein!*"

The frothing dogs stopped abruptly, panting, staring at the stranger beside their master. Their tongues fell out of their mouths in a pant. "They will only listen to me in German. That's how they're trained. Oh, and if you ever touch the perimeter wall, they are trained to attack to the death. I wouldn't test them."

Taylor nodded and sucked in the dry air.

"You must have a lot of questions," Dr. Kensington said.

Taylor was just happy not to be locked in the "White Room" anymore. She had not been outside in three days, and she had yet to see a single other patient at the rehab center.

Taylor and Dr. Kensington made their way 100 yards or so down the pathway to the wall's black metal gate. A winding roll of silver barbed wire lined the top and extended across the entire wall, topped by three parallel strings of prisonlike razor wire that reflected the sun. Dr. Kensington punched in a code. He held open the gate, allowing Taylor to enter first. She sensed his eyes tracking her body as she passed him, making her feel as if he was anything but a gentleman.

"Welcome to Casa Bell," Dr. Kensington said.

Neatly aligned squares of sandstone led the way to the front porch of the white stucco home. It was a cross between the opulent casas in the richest of her native Phoenix's old-money suburbs and that of historical Spanish-style missions. A bowling ball–sized bell dangled in a miniature tower that rose up from the center of the red-tile rooftop.

"Casa Bell is my residence, my sanctuary, and my laboratory." Dr. Kensington beamed. "That bell there, I take it you've heard it ringing."

"I have."

"Every hour on the hour—except for rest time. When you hear that bell at nine at night it's rest time. When it chimes at six it's work time."

Kee-kee-kee-kee! Kee-kee-kee-kee!

Taylor threw her hands in front of her face for protection as a creature rushed down the porch and charged at her.

"Rafferty! Settle down!" Dr. Kensington barked. He turned to Taylor. "Don't be afraid. That's just Rafferty."

The furry brown beast slid to a stop about six feet from

Taylor and let out a series of yelping barks. She now clearly saw it was a monkey wearing a human baby diaper.

"Get back here, you bad boy!" Dr, Kensington scolded.

He picked up the primate and carried him like a baby to the porch, grabbing a baby bottle filled with what looked like apple juice off the railing. When Dr. Kensington shook the bottle, Rafferty grabbed it violently and sucked the nipple. "You silly, silly boy. You need to listen to your daddy."

"How old is Rafferty, Dr. Kensington?" Taylor asked.

"Call me Peter."

"Okay, Peter . . ."

"Less than a year old. Rafferty is owned by one of our past Kensington patients. I'm, shall we say, monkey-sitting until he gets back from his, uh, time away. You have seen Rafferty in the media, I'm sure."

The only thing Taylor felt sure about was that this doctor gave her the creeps.

"Jason Wild, the pop singer, held him here as a pet," Peter said. "But as you have probably heard, it has been a rather tough year for Jason. Until he gets out of state prison, we are keeping Rafferty at Kensington."

"Jason was treated here?"

"Yes, but he was constantly resisting the Program, unfortunately. He's quite an intelligent and talented young man, so I expect him to come around in due time."

Due time. How much time she would be given before she was freed . . . or sent to prison, like Jason Wild? Either way, she needed to keep Peter on her good side.

Still holding the monkey, Peter settled into a rocking chair on the porch and gazed at her through his dark sunglasses.

"Why don't you join me?" Peter gestured to the empty rocking chair next to his. "I even have your favorite drink waiting for you."

Taylor took a seat and sipped from the glass of lemonade perched on the side table.

"You know, Taylor, we can learn a lot from primates," Peter said, stroking the monkey. "Chimps, monkeys, they are the closest species to human beings. Like humans, monkeys crave structure, order in their lives. They work best when there is a hierarchy in place. They like routine. They need to know who the alpha is, their leader."

Taylor put down her glass and wiggled in her chair, trying to get comfortable. She had spent so much time in bed over the last few days she couldn't twist her stiff neck without wincing.

"One thing you have to understand about monkeys is that your relationship with them is built totally on trust and respect," Peter continued. "Without that, they will reject your authority. For example, you can never hit a monkey. They will fear you and see you as a threat, not as their leader who will take care of them and protect them. The trick is winning their respect through discipline and punishment—without turning them against you."

Rafferty finished off the bottle and chucked it across the porch. It rolled off the ledge and into the yard. The monkey leaped off Peter's lap, straight onto the railing in front of Taylor, digging in the fingernails of his surprisingly humanlike black hands. Taylor gripped her chair. Rafferty belched a series of squeaks.

"Monkeys can smell fear. He's assessing you right now. That's why he's looking you straight in the eyes. You might want to stare back at him because if you look away, he might think you're submitting."

"Then what would happen?" Taylor locked eyes with the primate in front of her face.

"In the wild, he might gouge your eyes out." Peter laughed. "But luckily for you, this isn't the jungle. So he would probably just steal your glass of lemonade."

Act strong.

Peter laughed again, but Taylor did not. He went on, "The key is to assert your dominance through a simple system. When they do what you ask, you reward them. But when they don't, you punish them. It's really the natural order of things. Unfortunately, too many human parents forget this fundamental rule and that's partly why we have so many young children running wild. They do what they want, say what they want, act is if life is one big party. They reject authority. They don't respect order. Especially Hollywood kids."

Get control.

Since the news about Taylor's supposed rehab stint broke on *STARSTALK*, Brooklyn felt like she had to take charge of the situation.

Though it was possible Simone wasn't lying to her, she feared she'd been duped, misled, manipulated. Lied to! The sick feeling this gave her only had one remedy.

Brooklyn got up and ordered Holden to leave her house. "Now. Please, just go."

He did as she said and walked out the front door, no questions asked.

Then "it" began—the Fourmation.

She locked and unlocked the front door four times. Then she moved on to every doorknob in the house, twisting each four times, and counting out loud every time. She pressed the "4" button on the TV remote in the living room and arranged the bathroom in its proper order. She made sure the refrigerator temperature was set to "4" (it was) and pulled up the window shades in every room, leaving only four slats hanging down.

The Fourmation was the only thing that could prevent an inevitable calamity from occurring. Brooklyn's mom called it "OCD'ing." but Brooklyn preferred "prevention." No one understood the bullets she dodged by keeping her mind in order. No one ever could. Her system just worked.

A half hour or so later, with the Fourmation completed, Brooklyn placed four squirts of anti-bacterial lotion into her palm and rubbed her hands together, drying them with the friction. Only then did her heart stop its breathtaking palpitation.

Luckily she had never published any of the unverified lies Simone had given her. Very luckily. But regardless, *Deadline Diaries*, the supposed number-one online source of reporting on Taylor Prince for the last two years, had just been scooped by *STARSTALK*. And Brooklyn needed to right that wrong. ASAP.

She started by trying to confirm any details about Taylor's rehab stay with Taylor's publicist (no calls or emails returned) and the police (no record of visiting Taylor's address the night of her party).

Deadline Diaries fans, meanwhile, had assaulted her Twitter feed with questions, asking if the *STARSTALK* report were true. All Brooklyn could do was tweet:

> Regarding Taylor P News: DD is investigating. Story developing . . .

Blip, blip!

Brooklyn took her phone from her pocket and saw Simone's text.

> the STARSTALK story is fake. Totally. I swear!

> and why exactly should I believe u?

> because I am telling the Truth

When Brooklyn didn't reply, Simone continued her pleading.

> I know it looks bad, but Tay is NOT on drugs. Imposs! Trust me

> prove it

> how? I need YOU to prove it for me . . . u can confirm . . . it's ur job right?

Simone did have a point. She was just one single source after all. A big story would have legal ramifications if Brooklyn got it wrong and libeled someone, so she needed at least two independent sources.

Brooklyn had known this fundamental two-source rule since she was nine. Not from journalism school. Not from a textbook. Rather, from a movie.

Brooklyn's dad loved Robert Redford and the movie *All the President's Men*. Brooklyn and her dad had snuggled on the couch one night watching it on Netflix. "If I weren't a detective, I would have been a reporter," her dad told her. And since her dad insisted he would never allow her anywhere near guns, Brooklyn decided right then and there she would be a reporter when she grew up.

Now Brooklyn starred in her own drama. If she could get another source independent from Simone to verify her story, then she could possibly believe Simone.

Until then, however, she sent Simone a text back.

unsubstantiated gossip. sorry

fine. guess I'll just tip off
some other blogger . . .

Brooklyn didn't want to lose the story. She couldn't.

no. plz don't. just call me.

Twelve rings.

Dongggg. Dongggg. Dongggg. Dongggg.

The bell rang out from the apex of Casa Bell.

A self-satisfied smile on his face, Peter sat and drummed his fingers on his thigh in sync with each ring. Taylor couldn't take her eyes off the doctor's delicate, doll-like hands. His fingernails weren't the typical, stubby, male nails. Instead they were long and filed, jutting just beyond the fingertips, with perfectly smooth edges and a glossy sheen. They were as meticulously manicured as Taylor expected from a man who seemed obsessed with controlling every aspect of her life.

"Monkeys really are quite fascinating creatures," Peter said with a Michael Jackson–like babyishness. He clapped twice. Rafferty hopped from the top of the couch into Peter's arms. Peter stuck his forefinger into a jar of Nutella on the table in front of him and brought it to Rafferty's chattering teeth.

Rafferty leaned forward, wiping his tongue around Peter's finger and consuming every iota of the gooey treat within seconds.

Peter calmly shook his head, wagging his finger at the monkey. "Bad boy, you." Rafferty licked his tiny lips.

"I've found out where his least favorite place is. And when he doesn't listen to me or, say, eats his treat without me telling him to, he gets put there."

Peter stepped to the far corner of the room, baby-cradling Rafferty.

"His *cage.*"

Rafferty shook his brown head and placed his tiny hands over his eyes. His toylike hind legs trembled.

"The C-word," Peter said. "He absolutely despises the C-word."

Taylor wanted to tell Peter she believed humans were far more than hairless monkeys. She wanted to tell Peter he was a class-A creeper and needed to find a new hobby or just plain get a life. Or better yet, a wife. Or a husband. Anything would do! She so wanted to bust a heel into his groin. She visualized it. How satisfying it would be to knock the little man down, run for the door, scale the high compound walls, and escape to freedom.

But even Tae Kwon Do couldn't save her. Instead she would have to do the thing that had made her famous in the first place: act her way out of this mess.

"I couldn't agree with you more," Taylor said. She crossed her legs with interest.

"Oh, really?" Peter asked. "And exactly what part do you agree with?"

"That everyone needs a leader, a protector, a keeper. We as humans need smarter, more experienced leaders to help us through life."

Peter nodded. "Ahhh, you do?"

"I also agree wholeheartedly that punishment can help us learn from our mistakes."

Peter cracked a smile across his otherwise immobilized face.

"So, Taylor, tell me, do you have a mentor?" He leaned his chin on his folded hands.

"Several."

"That's just wonderful. Tell me who your mentors are."

"My mom and dad, they're mentors. They showed me the power of hard work and persistence. My sister, she has a disability—cerebral palsy. But her spirit to live is so strong. I definitely would consider her a mentor. And then there's my best friend, Simone. She's also my assistant, actually. She's a few years older than me, and I rely a lot on her because she has been through a lot of things."

"So you really consider *these people* mentors?" He laughed. "That's very cute."

"I'm sorry. I don't understand what—"

"You don't understand a lot, Ms. Prince. It would stand to reason that if you really had true mentors, people who were looking out for your best interests, you wouldn't be sitting here right now."

"No offense, Dr. Kensington, but—"

"Peter. Please, my dear, call me Peter."

"Okay, *Peter*, but how can I agree with you when no one has even explained to me why I'm here in the first place?"

"Ah yes, the reasons for your participation." He looked off the porch into the red rock garden.

More like confinement! Taylor bit down on her lip as a belt-long brown snake slithered in the gravel below.

"That is why I wanted to talk with you and get you out of that room," Peter said.

"You mean, my *cage*?"

"Ms. Prince, I don't know how many times I have to explain to you that I am here to help you. I am on your side. My goal—our goal—is to help you get well, to move on with your life in a healthy, pure, and infinitely non-toxic manner."

"Good. Then you can start helping me by explaining why I am caged up here like a monkey."

"Ms. Prince—"

"Call me *Taylor*."

Peter gritted his teeth. "Well, *Taylor*, you've been sent to Kensington because you're suffering from a host of mental health issues."

"Fascinating. Please continue."

"In addition to drug addiction, you have been diagnosed with delusional schizophrenia, not to mention instances of psychotic episodes featuring fits of violence against yourself and others. According to our evaluation, you are convinced that you are sober, but we have unearthed undeniable facts to the contrary. And the facts, I may add, are quite disturbing, particularly when you line them up with your complete and utter disconnection from the actual reality of your behavior. Kensington specializes in a new form of integrative therapy that will help you see true reality and detach from your projection of it."

Peter pulled out his cell phone, dialed a number, and put it to his ear. "Can you bring over Ms. Prince's report, please? Cheers, my friend."

Sliding the phone back into his pocket, he added, "Helper George is bringing over your report."

"By the way, I'm sorry about hitting George," Taylor said. "So if this is about my outburst, that is not at all normal behavior on my part. I apologize."

"George? He will be okay. Just a little swelling is all. As for you, we do need to work on your impulse control. I suppose we will add that to our to-do list. And my dear, it is quite a long list. And you have fourteen days of this 5250 hold to show some progress."

"5250?"

"The 5250 hold is what George was trying to explain when you opted to blame the messenger, so to speak, and viciously attack the man who was merely there to protect you from yourself."

The buzzer sounded and the front gate opened. Taylor watched George walk up the path to the main house. He had a square bandage stuck just above his right eye. He didn't look at Taylor as he cautiously walked up the stairs and handed Peter a folder. Taylor smiled—on the inside.

"Thank you, George," Peter said. "Before we go over the Program with Taylor, could you please explain to her the 5250 hold?"

"Of course, sir. It is, technically, Section 5250 of the California

Welfare and Institutions Code. This allows medical personnel or other qualified officers, such as ourselves, to involuntarily confine a person for up to fourteen days after they are held for seventy-two hours on the 5150 hold."

"And George, please tell her the criteria for a patient to be placed on such a hold."

"These holds, sir. They are reserved for patients who are deemed to have mental disorders that make them a danger to themselves and/or others."

"Tell me what happens after the fourteen days," Taylor said.

"You'll be free to go," Peter answered. "As long as you successfully complete the Program "

"And let's say for the sake of argument that I don't. Then what?"

"I wouldn't worry about that right now," Peter said. "From what I hear, you're a quick learner. A big part of living a life of wellness is learning to live in the moment."

Peter took a sip of lemonade and set it on the table. He took off his mirrored sunglasses. "You see, Taylor, statistics show that the leading causes of death are cancer and heart disease, but in truth, the number one cause of death is aging. Live long enough, and chances are you will develop a cancer. Or you will develop heart or respiratory problems. You know, Taylor, old people typically don't die from just being old. There is no such thing as chronological death. There is no ticking clock: there is no deadline to life. People usually die from something as simple as pneumonia because their lungs are so compromised, so weak from aging cells being broken down and degraded."

Taylor watched Peter's motionless cheeks, weirded out by how his mouth gaped open and shut like a ventriloquist dummy.

"The root cause of many addictions is the inability of people—especially teens—to cope with this. It's particularly hard for girls when they turn fifteen years old. They sense they are getting older, that their body is changing. Let's take you, for example. You may have already developed the first sign of wrinkles, or some thigh or belly fat. Perhaps you are getting a neurotic sense that you are marching toward death and life is no longer something in your control. Simply put, you aren't ready to grow up. This, I've concluded, causes an overall state of anxiety, an unease that pushes many people to escape through various drugs or alcohol. It truly is an epidemic—a sad, sad trend. And it needs to be treated because teens are tomorrow's adults, and they will shape the future of our species. Especially influential teens like you, Taylor. You have a great opportunity to not only help yourself, but to show others the proper path. The infinite path."

Taylor felt her heart race as Peter wagged his forefinger like a preacher.

"So I ask you this: If religion and twelve-step programs offer real cures for such deadly maladies, then why are the rates of addiction on the rise?" Peter's voice rose to the point just below shouting. "Because those programs, those supposed paths to healing, do not address the aging issues I have laid out to you. That, my young friend, is the truth. But, Taylor, that's why we call *my* program '*the* Program.' It only works if you are fully committed to it. Only then will the infinite purity of youth heal you. Forever."

Taylor didn't move from her chair.

Just act.

"Sounds good," Taylor finally said. "Once I complete the Program I can spread the word."

"Are you prepared to make the necessary changes in your life so that you can heal yourself and inspire the world? Are you prepared to commit fully—and I mean *fully*—to the Program?"

"Yes," she said solemnly. "I am."

"Very good then."

Peter stood and grabbed Rafferty by the hand. "You're a very smart girl, Taylor. I had a feeling you would get it, and I trust that you aren't just saying this to appease me." Rafferty jumped into his arms. "It will take a lot of work. Everyone wants the quick fix in life these days. But it takes commitment and integrity, Taylor. And it requires a leader to step up and show you the way."

Kee-kee-kee-kee. Kee-kee-kee-kee.

"Rafferty, calm down!" The hyperactive monkey leaped from Peter's arms and squatted on the porch, scratching his stomach.

"My friend here is getting hungry," Peter said. "So I will leave you with George. Before we can start on our path, the next step is signing your commitment papers. George will handle the paperwork. And once you sign, I'll be your leader. I will have control of your legal, professional, and personal affairs. Then, and only then, can we promptly get you back on track. You merely have to trust me and the process. The results, I promise you, will be transformative."

"But I can't sign something like that. That's like signing my life away."

Peter shrugged. "The way I see it, there's not much of a life waiting for you out there."

Taylor could feel the same bubbling rage that had landed her in the padded room.

"Helper George," Peter said, "please explain to Taylor the depth of her problems. Rafferty here needs a little snacky-snack."

Peter turned and carried the monkey into the house.

"Ms. Prince," George said wearily. "The news is not good."

"I know," Simone said. "It sounds shady, but you gotta believe me!"

"Beyond shady," Brooklyn said, rolling her eyes at Simone through the phone. "And, no, I don't have to believe you."

"Taylor was not on drugs. And Taylor did *not* try to kill herself! She also didn't shave her head—there's no way! That *STARSTALK* story is fake, total fiction."

"Simone, I really want to believe you. I like you. But I need more proof. I mean, they have a picture of her shaved head! It's all over the web! And it looks legit."

"I realize that, but . . . look, no offense, but do I have to go tell another blogger?"

"Even if you go calling some other journalist, they're going to need the same thing from you—I mean, if they are credible. So at this point, maybe you should just go to the cops if you really think Taylor has been taken against her will or has been kidnapped or whatever. Just go and report her missing. Because honestly, if I were to post a story right now saying that she was missing or kidnapped and that the *STARSTALK* story was false, even suggesting it—with no verified evidence—I would be laughed off the Internet."

"But I can't go to the cops right now because—"

"Because you're afraid you'll get arrested. I get it. The bottom line is that I don't have the facts to back up your kidnapping theory. Like we would go to the cops and say, 'Even though it looks like an intervention and there is a report she is in rehab, we think she was kidnapped, but we have no idea where she is or who took her and, we have, oh, zero proof?' But, hey, feel free to call the police if you feel like it's a last resort."

"Okay, okay," Simone said. "You and I both know we can't go to the cops yet. And you—"

"What about me?"

"You'd rather break a story than hand the cops a case."

Brooklyn slid her baseball cap around backward. "You really don't know a damn thing about me, do you?"

"If you really knew *me* you wouldn't accuse me of lying."

"I am not saying you're lying. All right, maybe at first I did think you were lying. But can you blame me for thinking that?"

"No, I totally realize how insane this all seems."

"But this story isn't about me or you. It's about the truth and about finding Taylor," Brooklyn said.

"I don't know what else I can do."

"Well, I have some ideas."

"Okay, like?"

"You could find that pretty boy from the party. You know, your drug buddy. If anyone at that party was involved in snatching her, he would seem to be the prime suspect."

Brooklyn's father would have called Pretty Boy a "person of interest"—a suspicious person who seemed like he knew more than the facts at hand. In Brooklyn's investigative journalist lingo, she called him a "primary source."

"Can you track the dude down?" Brooklyn asked.

"I already gave you his number," Simone said. "Can't you trace it?"

"I've tried. No luck. So far, at least."

"Should we just call him?"

"I've tried that, too. It doesn't pick up and has no voicemail. He obviously has your number, so he might pick up if you call. Or you can text him. It's worth a shot. I mean, time is running out."

"What do you mean?"

"If that *STARSTALK* story is fake, and Taylor really was

taken against her will, that can't be a good thing. She could be in danger."

"Okay, okay, fine." Simone sighed. "I'll try to find the guy and see if he knows anything. But can't you just call rehabs and see if Taylor's a patient anywhere? Won't they tell you?"

"It's not that easy. But I'm working on it. I'm doing *my* job. Now you can help me, and help Taylor, by doing *your* job."

Their phone chat fell into awkward silence. Brooklyn filled it.

"That thing you said about me wanting to break a story more than letting the cops get the credit?"

"Yeah?"

"My dad investigated crimes for over twenty years. Murders, robberies, rapes, assaults, even kidnappings. And he solved most of them. Rarely did he ever get credit. And never did he send a case to his bosses or to the D.A. without knowing in his heart that what he was reporting was total truth."

"Sounds like a great man," Simone said sincerely.

"All I'm doing is my best to live up to his standard. I don't need credit. My ego doesn't need attention. You're the one who pointed out that I never post pictures of myself on Instagram. That's because I don't want to be the story, I want the truth to be the story."

"I apologize for—"

"Are you at a computer?" Brooklyn asked.

"Staring at my laptop as we speak."

"If there's ever any doubt about my intentions, just go to the top of the *Deadline Diaries* home page and click on 'TIPS.'"

Brooklyn could hear Simone tapping her keyboard. "When you click on it, what appears at the top of the page?"

Simone replied, "There's a quote from Henry David Thoreau. 'Rather than love, than money, than fame, give me truth.'"

"Well, Georgie." Taylor crossed her pajama-covered legs after settling onto the padded porch chair next to the Helper. "Before you start telling me how much of a mess I am in again, can you promise to get me some real clothes?"

"Yes," George said. "We can arrange that."

"My stylist always says, 'Look good, feel good, do good.' A girl needs to look good, even in rehab. These baggy things don't exactly show off my assets."

George reached inside a cardboard box that had been sitting beside his feet. "We don't have a stylist on staff, but we do have a PW."

"A what?"

"Program Wardrobe. Now that we have your measurements . . ." The Helper pulled out a stack of clothes and handed it to Taylor. She inspected each item, of which there were three sets: Black yoga pants, black workout tights, black leggings, a forest-green Lycra top, and a matching green jog bra. A green square label with "∞2∞" was stitched on a tag in each piece of clothing.

"How did you get my measurements?" Taylor asked.

"Our staff handled that when you were admitted."

She blocked her chest with her arms. "While I was unconscious?"

"They took care of you in a professional manner, I assure—"

"That is beyond wrong and creepy!" Taylor said as she read the tag on a bra. "Not that it's any of your business, but I'm a C. This size small will flatten me like a pancake!"

"Doctor Kensington would like you to put on your wardrobe."

She placed her hands on her hips and glared.

"It's mandatory," he said firmly.

"Fine. Turn around."

George turned his back to Taylor, looking sheepishly at his clipboard as she quickly slid out of her pajamas and into the yoga pants, bra, and top.

"There are running shoes in the box," George said, blindly pointing behind himself with his thumb.

She stretched out the band of the tight-fitting bra. "Okay, I'm decent."

He turned around, unclipped a document at least twenty pages thick from his clipboard, and handed it to her. "This is the contract Peter mentioned."

"First of all," Taylor said, "Dr. Kensington told me you could explain the so-called 'depth of my problems.' Before I sign anything, can we start there?"

"Okay." George opened a manila folder. "You are facing serious charges."

He slipped out an official-looking document and gave it to her. A large black metal paper clip held it together.

SUPERIOR COURT OF THE STATE OF CALIFORNIA
FOR THE COUNTY OF LOS ANGELES

THE PEOPLE OF THE STATE OF CALIFORNIA
Plaintiff Name

Case No. XX

_____
D.A. Complainant's Signature

v.

TAYLOR PRINCE
Defendant Name

_____
Judge Ronald Opin Signature

CRIMINAL COMPLAINT

I, the complainant in this case, state that the following is true to the best of my knowledge and belief.

On or about the date of August 2 in the County of Los Angeles in the State of California the defendant violated:

> **Code Section: Health & Safety Code 11350 HS/11351 HS/11364 HS/11364 HS**

> **Offense Description:** Possession of a Controlled Substance/Possession for Sale of Narcotics

This criminal complaint is based on the following facts:

On or about August 2, a lawful search and seizure of a home at 458 Nichols Canyon, Los Angeles, CA 90046 [The Residence], found more than 1,000 grams of heroin in a closet in an upstairs bedroom of The Residence. It has been determined that The Residence is owned and occupied by Taylor Prince [Defendant]. Upon further investigation of the premises, more than $200,000 in cash was found in the bedroom of Defendant, as well as paraphernalia used for the delivery of heroin into the body. After interviews with eyewitnesses, and upon discovery of the aforementioned items, it has been determined that Defendant possessed the narcotic with the intent and purpose of use and sale. **Health & Safety Code 11350** makes it a felony to possess narcotics such as cocaine, crack, and heroin. **Health & Safety Code 11351** makes it a felony to possess illegal drugs for the purpose of selling them. **Health & Safety Code 11364** makes it a misdemeanor to possess "an opium pipe or any device, contrivance, instrument, or paraphernalia used for unlawfully injecting or smoking a controlled substance." Upon questioning during the raid, Defendant stated that the drugs were in fact in her possession. As such, the District Attorney for the County of Los Angeles [The People] has found sufficient evidence to charge Defendant with two felony counts in violation of 11350 HS and 11351 HS and one misdemeanor count in violation of 11364 HS. Further, The People seek a warrant for the arrest of Defendant and ask that court officers remand Defendant into custody, without bail, in the Los Angeles Juvenile Detention Center upon the signing of this complaint by a Judge.

Taylor read the court document several times over as George sat beside her in silence. She struggled to catch her breath.

"I don't understand," was all she could muster.

"I know it's a lot to take in." George carefully placed his hand on the back of her shoulder and patted her. "But this is what the doctor was referring to. These are, obviously, very serious charges, and we are here to make this go away."

"But they aren't even true." Taylor dropped the papers onto the porch. "It's not true. Just not true."

George took the pile of papers and shuffled them into order. Taylor kept shaking her head in disbelief.

"I understand the shock you are probably in," he said. "But you are a very lucky young lady. You must have some friends in very high places. If you are convicted of these crimes, depending on how much the judge thinks celebrities are spoiled brats, you could face more than several years in prison. But you are lucky. Because the criminal complaint has not been signed yet."

"Let me see," Taylor said, pulling the paper from his hands, scanning to the end. "Why not?"

"Because someone wanted to give you a chance at redemption. And Kensington is the only place that can save you." He placed the contract in her lap. It looked legit. "Just sign here. Think about it. Do you really have any other choice?"

James Bond. When Brooklyn's phone jingled alive with the old-school *007* theme song, it meant only one person calling. She stuffed in her earbuds.

"What's up, Holds?"

"Bad news," Holden said.

"Hit me. Things can't get much worse."

"It's Simone Witten."

"And?"

"She's a convicted felon."

"You kidding me?" Brooklyn squeezed her phone like a stress ball.

"Actually, I should say that Simone *White* is a felon. White is her legal name. Witten is just an alias."

Brooklyn stomped on her bedroom's floor. "You. Are. Kidding."

"It's for real. I cross-referenced her name in a tracking database and found both names connected to her residential address. Then I did a Lexis search under Simone White and found she has two convictions in California. One for felony shoplifting, and the other for armed robbery. I just emailed you the court docs."

"Wow. But now everything makes total sense!"

"That she's a liar?"

"No. I mean, yeah. I didn't ever really get why Simone didn't go to the cops. She claimed it was due to the drugs in the house. But Simone came to me because she already has two strikes against her."

"Strikes?'"

"The three-strikes law," Brooklyn explained with forced patience. "In California, when a person commits three serious felonies, they can be automatically sentenced to twenty-five years in a state prison. My dad loved that law because it's meant to scare the crap out of criminals. And since she already admitted to me she had drugs on her that night, she probably freaked out about getting her third strike."

Brooklyn couldn't help but think about her dad, Detective Kit Brant. Most aspiring cops majored in criminal justice, but her dad had also double-majored in psychology because he believed solving crimes began with understanding the criminal mind. Though always quick to point out "you can't arrest someone for having a thought," her father psychologically profiled every suspect for possible motivations or factors that may have driven them to commit a crime. Brooklyn was now determined to do the same.

"So now what?" Holden asked.

"I break the story that Taylor's assistant is a convicted felon."

"But I thought *Taylor* was the story. Does anyone really care about Simone?"

"If they don't now, they certainly will after this. *Deadline Diaries* needs to compete on this Taylor story, Holden. It may not be the biggest angle on the story, but it's something to show my readers that I am on top of it while I try to figure out exactly what is going on." She sighed. "Plus, think about Taylor. The poor girl could be . . ."

"You think someone killed her?"

"I don't know. But maybe breaking this story will smoke out another source. We have to try."

"Brooklyn, maybe we should just file a report with the cops."

"No. I don't trust them. I think they were in on it." Brooklyn began tapping on her keyboard. "First, I have to get a comment from Simone. It might force her to cough up more information."

"The cops are behind Taylor's disappearance? That doesn't make sense. Simone said they didn't look like the cops when they—"

"Simone, exactly. The one who has already lied to us."

Brooklyn hadn't even hung up on Holden when she began writing up the story in her blogging program.

HEADLINE:

DD EXCLUSIVE: TAYLOR PRINCE ASSISTANT CONVICTED FELON, RAISES QUESTIONS ABOUT TAYLOR'S LIFE BEFORE ALLEGED MENTAL BREAKDOWN

BODY TEXT:

Deadline Diaries has exclusively learned that actress Taylor Prince's longtime personal assistant and confidante, Simone Witten, 20, is, in fact, a convicted felon who has been arrested for shoplifting and armed robbery. In court documents obtained exclusively by *Deadline Diaries*, we've learned her legal name is Simone White, and she was convicted of stealing $10,000 worth of merchandise from a downtown Los Angeles clothing store, as well as serving as an accomplice to an armed robbery of an L.A.-area convenience store. Both arrests occurred prior to Simone becoming Prince's assistant. It's not yet known whether Prince knew of Witten's troubled past.

News of Witten's criminal background could possibly shed light on Prince's private life leading up to her alleged mental breakdown and reported **stint in rehab** following her sixteenth birthday party last week. (*Deadline Diaries* has not yet confirmed reports of Taylor's rehab.)

When contacted for comment on our story, Witten told *Deadline Diaries*: XXXXXX

After Brooklyn clicked Save, she immediately texted Simone so she could fill in the "XXXXXX."

> hey, Ms. WHITE = running a DD story on ya: 1) ur a convicted felon 2) 'Witten' is an alias and ur name is WHITE. what comment, if any, do you have, Ms. WHITE?

Brooklyn realized that, legally speaking, she could run the story without a comment since she already had an official court document to back up her reporting. But out of fairness and professional ethics as a journalist, she felt she owed it to Simone to give her a chance to comment.

Brooklyn didn't want to be yet another cheesy, sell-out celeb "news" site. Several brand marketing people had approached her about writing "sponsored posts" for different products—from cell phones to zit cream to backpacks—where they would pay her $200 a mention. But she had always said no. She wanted to maintain integrity.

Whenever she was frustrated by not having a fully staffed news organization at her disposal, she recalled "The Talk," the one-on-one meeting with the school counselor that frayed the nerves of every Twin Oaks junior. It was the meeting where college dreams could be crushed or inspired.

"I get that my grades aren't that awesome, but who wouldn't want a world-famous investigative blogger attending their journalism school?" Brooklyn had asked Mr. Watts.

"Well, Columbia University," Mr. Watts replied. "And Northwestern. And USC. You're applying to all the best schools, and all will require a higher GPA and higher SAT scores."

"How high?" Brooklyn asked.

Mr. Watts gazed over his glasses at her academic report. Then he looked up. "Brooklyn, I must be honest with you. The fact is that you have a lot of work ahead of you in order to get into an elite institution. Your GPA is currently at 3.7 but must come up to 4.0 to be taken seriously. On the plus side, your SAT scores show great promise. You have a 720 on Writing and a 707 on the Critical Reading, which are both competitive. But your math . . ."

Brooklyn swallowed whatever saliva remained in her mouth.

"A 580 is just not going to cut it," he said. "You need closer to 700. Much closer."

"But most professional journalists don't even use math, and when they do, they probably just use a calculator."

"Perhaps. But these are the rules."

"But you said extracurricular activities, like my blog, are considered as factors for admission. Couldn't *Deadline Diaries* somehow make up for my math scores?"

"It would be a factor in their admissions decision. But I've never seen a student with your numbers get into any of those schools, even with excellent additional materials."

"Even a Pulitzer?"

"I'm sorry?"

"Did any of those high school students ever win a Pulitzer?"

"If you're referring to the Pulitzer Prize, for the world's best journalism, then no, they did not. It would be a first for a high school student to even be nominated for a Pulitzer Prize, let alone win one."

That was six months ago. Now, just a month away from becoming a senior and a few months from taking another SAT, the reality remained that Brooklyn wasn't much of a test taker, especially when it came to math. No matter how many tutoring sessions she did, solving equations of most any kind proved frustrating. She would somehow want to see the "fours" in every problem, a mental tic that created yet another problem-within-a-problem. In trig, whenever she saw $y = 3x$, she would immediately think, obsessively, that $x = 4$. Thus, $y = 3(4) = 12$. But when her teacher informed her that, say, $x = 7$, she would have to divide the subsequent answer by 4 after solving the original problem. Just because . . . well, she had to.

As she waited for Simone to respond to her text, Brooklyn went back to reporting out the other angles of the Taylor Prince story. The list of things she didn't know was a lot longer than the list of things she did know. Besides Simone being a felon with a fake name, she had yet to confirm the most important angle. Had Taylor really been admitted to rehab for drug problems or was the *STARSTALK* story yet another fine example of their tabloid fiction? And since it was widely known in celebrity journalism circles that the majority of *STARSTALK*'s stories were fed to them by police sources, could the cops somehow be complicit in a conspiracy?

Hunches. That's all they were.

Several times, Brooklyn had called the number she found in Arizona for Taylor's mom, but the phone just rang out before assaulting her ears with a busy signal. And Taylor's publicist, manager, and agent had not returned any of her emails or calls. Even her usual go-to source for celebrity sightings—Twitter and Instagram—had nothing to report on Taylor's whereabouts.

Brooklyn knew that the stories most worth pursuing were the hardest to break. Like her math scores, she would just have to dig deeper to overcome the challenge.

Batman had Robin. Woodward paired up with Bernstein. Ramona had Beezus. And Brooklyn had Holden.

> Hey, Holdy. Wanna come over tonite?
> MUST brainstorm, need a reporting plan.
> You in?

> Sure. C u in a bit

A choice. George told Taylor she didn't have one. Technically, though, she did. She could, for example, plot an escape, but then she'd run the risk of getting chewed alive by German shepherds or mauled by a hyper monkey. She could opt out and not sign the contract that George had placed before her. But the choice between facing years in prison on felony charges (a PR nightmare) and hopefully getting the criminal charges dropped and wiped from her record seemed pretty clear.

Taylor took hold of George's pen, and after letting out a here-goes-nothing exhale, scrawled her autograph with her trademark giant T and P followed by a series of squiggles.

"Legally the state of California now considers Dr. Peter Kensington your conservator," George said, placing the document into his folder. "This means Peter can make all decisions—personal, medical, and professional—on your behalf."

Taylor had heard about these conservatorships. It's what parents of the most train-wrecked celebrities usually obtained. *Am I that crazy?*

"What about my mother? Doesn't she have to sign off?"

"She has granted Dr. Kensington power of attorney," George said. "He has explained your difficult predicament to her. She trusts him."

"Can I speak to her?"

"Upon completion of the Program." George stood up. "So let's not waste any more time. Come with me."

As she followed George out of Casa Bell across the courtyard and back to the clinic, Taylor looked up at the midday blue sky and basked in the warmth of a sun she had seen very little of over the last few days. When she stepped back into the clinic the AC-cooled air sent a shiver through her.

George pushed open a door directly across the hall from the padded room. Inside stood Dr. Kensington, pacing with his arms crossed at the far end of the room. He smiled when he saw Taylor. He nodded to George, who left, closing the door behind him.

"Dr. Kensington." Taylor nodded in return.

"Call me Peter, my child," he said. "Here, have a seat."

Taylor sat at the long oak table in the middle of the classroom, which was one of only six rooms in the single-story adobe casita that constituted the "clinic." The other rooms were her bedroom, the examination room, the exercise room, the kitchen, and the infamous padded white room. It was like a high-end Palm Springs spa resort—except for the being-held-against-your-will part.

"You will no doubt become the healthiest you have ever been in your life," Peter told her. "You will gain clarity. You will feel a youthful vigor. In just a few days, you will have never felt more vital, more alive. You will experience a purity of body, mind, and spirit."

Taylor looked out the window at the heat ripples hovering above the desert.

"But you can only get better by living better," Peter continued. "Do you realize that almost every fatal illness one gets with aging can be prevented with proper diet? The mainstream medical community has brainwashed us into believing it is pills that prevent and cure diseases. But the truth is, by the time you need to take a pill it is too late. By then you've aged, you've developed terminal diseases, and your immune system has been compromised."

He proudly held up a laminated, iPhone-size cardboard square and set it on the table in front of her. "This, my dear, is a very short guide to a very long and happy life. You will carry this with you always."

Taylor picked up the card, reading the first few lines silently.

"Please, my child," Peter said. "Go ahead and read the list out loud."

Taylor swallowed hard, then did as instructed.

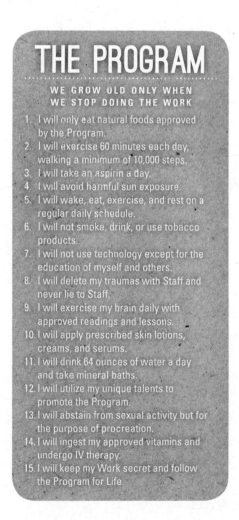

THE PROGRAM

WE GROW OLD ONLY WHEN
WE STOP DOING THE WORK

1. I will only eat natural foods approved by the Program.
2. I will exercise 60 minutes each day, walking a minimum of 10,000 steps.
3. I will take an aspirin a day.
4. I will avoid harmful sun exposure.
5. I will wake, eat, exercise, and rest on a regular daily schedule.
6. I will not smoke, drink, or use tobacco products.
7. I will not use technology except for the education of myself and others.
8. I will delete my traumas with Staff and never lie to Staff.
9. I will exercise my brain daily with approved readings and lessons.
10. I will apply prescribed skin lotions, creams, and serums.
11. I will drink 64 ounces of water a day and take mineral baths.
12. I will utilize my unique talents to promote the Program.
13. I will abstain from sexual activity but for the purpose of procreation.
14. I will ingest my approved vitamins and undergo IV therapy.
15. I will keep my Work secret and follow the Program for Life.

Taylor looked up at Peter. "This is it?"

He patted her on the back. "Easy as pie."

"This is all I have to do?"

"The Program will teach you that all the enlightenment and fulfillment one needs can be found by following these fifteen rules. Human beings like to make things more complicated than they need to be, my child."

"It's me!" Holden shouted from Brooklyn's front doorstep. "Open up!"

Brooklyn opened the front door. "Dude." She glanced at her phone. "It's been almost four hours."

"I drove as fast as I could," Holden huffed, pushing his glasses up and closing the door behind him. "I had to clean my room first. My mom freaks out when I don't."

"Why's she so obsessed?"

He shrugged. "It's a Korean thing?"

"Okay, Mr. Racist," Brooklyn said.

"Hey, you can't be racist if you're talking about your own race," he shot back. "My dad's always claiming our rules are 'a Korean thing,' as if that justifies everything. Like having to keep the house as clean as an operating room."

"But isn't your dad a surgeon?"

"Yeah."

"So then it's also a doctor thing."

"Brooklyn, where are you going with this?"

"I'm saying that cleanliness and order is a *good* thing. I'm the only one in my house who freaks out when things aren't in order. Actually, my mom wishes I didn't clean so much. She's the messy one I'm always cleaning up after."

"I'm glad you brought that up."

"What?"

"Your whole organizing thing," Holden said. "Like when you kicked me out earlier so you could do that fours thing that you do."

"How do you know what I did after you left?"

"When you slammed the door I could hear you lock and unlock the door—four times—while I was still standing on the porch."

"So you creeped on me," she said, walking away.

"Listening is hardly creeping."

"What business is it of yours anyway? Are you going to be all like my mom now and tell me I need to see a shrink?"

"No, Brooklyn. I've known you since sixth grade. Trust me, I'm fully aware that no one can tell you what to do."

"Then why are you even bringing this up, especially right now?"

"Because I think it's getting in the way of your life. I read an article today saying that when a compulsion interferes with daily life it has become a problem that needs treatment. You've even told me you have trouble with math because you have to—"

"Okay, Dr. Phil! If I want to be preached at, I'll go to church."

Brooklyn turned down the hall.

Holden followed. "You don't need to overreact, Brooklyn. The whole fours thing is not necessary. That's all I am saying. Honestly, I don't even understand why you would pick four of all numbers. In Korea, four is an *unlucky* number. If anything, you should do sevens."

Brooklyn stopped at her bedroom door. "I called you over to help me break this story, not to psychoanalyze me, you weirdo. On top of that, I'm fine. Or at least I was until you came over here and started judging me." She planted a couple light taps on his cheek with an open hand. "As a matter of fact, I don't need your help. I have my own computer. I can handle it from here. You're not needed."

"So that's what I am to you?" Holden snapped. "A computer?"

"No. That's not it." Her lips pursed into a pout. She felt guilty. "Actually, I do need you."

"As a friend, or an assistant?"

"Honestly, both. If you haven't noticed, I don't exactly have a ton of friends these days."

This was true. The more time she dedicated to her blogging,

the more Brooklyn's social world had shrunk—"isolated" is how her mother put it.

Holden slid his hands in his pockets and shrugged. "You sure have an interesting way of showing your friendship."

"Hey, I'm a work in progress. Maybe it's just part of being in high school. Nobody's perfect."

"I still think we had a perfect relationship."

"Holds, we've talked about this. We weren't perfect. We aren't meant to be that way. Perfect friends, yes. Lovers, not so much."

Holden shook off her comment with a nod. "I know, I know . . ."

Brooklyn had been the one to break up with Holden, even though they told their friends it was "mutual" in order to avoid drama. But they both knew the truth: she dumped him. Brooklyn had sat him down three months into dating and informed him that he was way too important to her as a friend to risk losing him if they got too serious romantically and ended up broken up. In Brooklyn's head, it was simply a preventative measure.

Before she could re-explain her reasoning for their split, Brooklyn's FaceTime rang on her phone.

"Hello?" she answered. Holden rolled his eyes.

"Brooklyn!" Simone was sitting outside on a patio looking haggard compared to the other day at the stadium.

"Ms. White? Or is it Witten?"

"C'mon, hear me out," she pleaded. "Okay, all that stuff about me and my past is true. But Taylor knows everything about me. I just changed my name to get a fresh start."

Brooklyn sat down at her desk. "So you're confirming my story?"

"Yes, sort of," Simone said. "But I swear that everything else I told you about Taylor is also true. She was taken. I'm telling you, this is not at all what it looks like."

Brooklyn flashed a puke face into the camera. "We're going in circles here."

"But I have proof."

"Okay . . ."

Simone stuck a cigarette in her mouth and took a puff. "Surveillance video. From Taylor's house." She blew out the smoke. "I found it."

"You went back to her house?"

"I'm here now."

"But I told you to lay low and stay away from there. Someone could be on to you."

"Yeah, well, you also said you were about to out me as a felon. But I remembered she had a surveillance system, and I just checked it. There's video of those guys taking her! You'll see that everything I said is totally true."

"Okay. So then just bring me the tape."

"That's the problem," Simone said. "It's not a tape, *per se*. It's just video on a monitor. I don't know how to save it onto a drive or anything. I could maybe figure it out, but it will take time. Why don't you come down to the house?"

"Just FaceTime me the video from your phone."

"I would, but this is literally the only place at her house I can get reception."

"How about Wi-Fi?"

"Taylor had it turned off when she got into her yoga phase. She wanted to make this place a sanctuary."

Brooklyn glanced at her phone. It was 4:22 p.m. Her mom wouldn't approve of her heading down to L.A., but then again, she wouldn't be home from work until after ten o'clock.

"I don't own a car. Actually, I don't even drive." She batted her eyes over at Holden. "But I might be able to get a ride from *someone*."

Holden, off camera, shook his head "no."

"Simone, hold on a sec," Brooklyn said, pressing Mute and pointing the camera at the floor.

"Holden, this is a huge. If I see footage of her being taken away, that's a huge story, total confirmation. Right? I have to see this video."

Holden shot her a blank stare.

Brooklyn unmuted. "Text me the address. I'll find a way to get there."

She hung up and took the glasses off Holden's face and put them on her own. "Holden, Holden, Holden. You know, glasses can be quite sexy, don't ya think."

Holden snatched his glasses off her face and put them back on. "Stop it, Brooklyn. You're making a huge mistake."

"Wearing glasses?" she joked.

"I don't trust that girl Simone at all. She's sketchy."

"Sure, she is. But she also could be telling the truth. She didn't deny her shady past—she confirmed it! If every source had to be an angel, journalists would hardly ever break a story."

Brooklyn clutched Holden's forearm. "C'mon. You're a smart guy. The smartest person I know. That's what I love about you." She adjusted his glasses again. "But you're also a safe guy. Too safe."

"You say that like it's a bad thing to not want to die."

"It's also a bad thing to not want to live. I'd rather die young for exposing the truth than live forever for ignoring it."

Holden guided her hand over her heart. "You need to learn when to think with this." He then placed her hand on her forehead. "And when to use this."

Brooklyn wanted to grab him by his cute, unblemished face and kiss him—four times—on the lips. Just like when they were boyfriend and girlfriend. Just like when she had thought having a boyfriend would make her a happier person. Perhaps four kisses would persuade Holden to change his mind, and make her one less lonely girl. But then . . .

"Think about your dad," he said.

She backed away. "What about him?"

"He wouldn't want you to go. And you know it."

She stepped back. "My dad's not here."

"Maybe because he took a risk that day."

"He died doing what he loved." Brooklyn blinked back tears.

"He also broke a department rule by meeting with a potential witness alone," Holden said. "It proved deadly."

Brooklyn ran her fingers through her hair and wet her lips. "I can stay up here in this little Twin Oaks bubble my whole life and play it safe and never go anywhere, never take a chance, like everyone else at our school probably will their entire lives. I could get a job with the oil company or teach grade school or work at Target. But I refuse to let fear of something possibly bad happening stop me from making a better life for myself."

"So you're willing to lose your life?"

Brooklyn stepped closer to Holden. "Do you want to be one of the safe, boring people, Holden? Do you want to be the perfect boring student who does perfect boring things, so you can go get a perfectly boring job and live a perfectly uninspired life? Because I, for one, don't want to be that person. I want to make a difference, I want to live a life of adventure. I want to open people's eyes to injustice, truth, different perspectives. I want to feel fulfilled. And I bet you a million dollars that I will never feel fulfilled if I never leave my bedroom."

Holden stared silently.

"Seriously, Holden. What are you going to do with your life?"

"You know the answer," he replied.

"Oh, that's right, *games*. You want to design video games. Silly, pointless games. You want to create things for people that divert them from reality. Well, that's not me. I want to draw people into reality, expose reality, enhance people's lives by breaking stories that reveal truth."

"No offense, but I don't think picking through celebrity trash is exactly making a difference in people's lives."

"Hey, you gotta start somewhere. And, by the way, Hollywood matters because it's a business about portraying fantasy. There's nothing more important than dreams and imagination. Dreams are what keep you going when everyone else has stopped believing."

Holden went to hug her.

Brooklyn turned away. "It's not like I'm some pseudo blogger on Tumblr spreading gossip and lies. I have ethics, standards. Yes, I cover entertainment and celebrities. But celebrities have a social currency that can be as valuable as any politician. Look at George Clooney and his work in Africa. Angelina's volunteering to help refugees with the U.N. Demi Lovato got people talking about body image, drug addiction, and eating disorders with girls. But the messed up part is that celebrity-focused journalism has become a dying art. And you know what? I want *Deadine Diaries* to be the authority. That's *my* dream."

Brooklyn reached into the top drawer of her nightstand and pulled out a notecard. "At my dad's funeral, my grandmother gave me this. My dad kept it in his desk at work."

Holden read the typewritten text. "'There are just some kind of men . . . who're so busy worrying about the next world they've never learned to live in this one.' It's from *To Kill a Mockingbird*."

Brooklyn took the card back and read the reverse side aloud. "'Most men lead lives of quiet desperation and go to the grave with the song still in them.' Henry David Thoreau. My dad didn't want to be that guy who didn't get the most out of life. And that's how he lived until that day."

"Which day?" Holden asked.

"The day he died."

"I know, but what *date* was it?"

"April fourth."

"So it was four-four?"

"Yes, Holden. It was four-four."

"So the Fourmation comes from—"

"The worst day of my life? Yes, it does. Congrats. You cracked the code."

Brooklyn sat on her bed and slid on her sneakers. "Holden, I really can't get into this right now. We can talk in the car, I promise. But it's almost five o'clock and we've got to get going. I swear I'll be extra careful."

"No. I can't be a part of this. It's too risky, and my mom and dad would kill me. Sorry, but I can't."

Brooklyn tied her last sneaker lace tightly and stood up. She walked to her closet and pulled out her favorite red-and-black flannel shirt. "Okay, fine. Don't go with me. You're right. It's not the safe thing. But I know someone who's not afraid."

Holden made the palms-out stop sign with both his hands. "Don't. Please. Do not call *her*."

Brooklyn placed the call. She waited a few seconds for it to connect.

"Hey, Tamara!" she said brightly. "Wanna go to L.A.?"

Fifteen rules. Taylor studied the list after Peter left her alone in her room to memorize it.

Some of the rules seemed reasonable, the kinds of things a health-conscious person would appreciate. She could not, for example, argue it was bad to stay out of the sun (her mom had preached sunscreen her entire childhood in Arizona), take a daily aspirin, eat healthy, sleep well, and abstain from smoking or doing drugs. But she thought the stuff about not having sex (even though she wasn't active herself at the moment), sharing "traumas" with staff, submitting to "IV therapy," and, oh, following the Program *for life* sounded straight out of some kind of freakish cult.

"Is this, like, a religion or something?" Taylor asked Peter when he returned a while later.

Peter laughed. "No, no, no, my dear. Religion is for the ignorant. The Program is for the intelligent and informed."

"Good," Taylor said. "I thought for a second this was a cult or something."

"Religion is the product of ancient fantasy and myth. Those who practice religion put faith in entirely unproven concepts, yet they convince themselves it will bring them enlightenment, or salvation, or deliver them to some afterlife and grant them immortality. My years of research show that the only way we as a species can approach anything close to immortality is by simply doing the Work."

Taylor nodded, not in agreement but in fear.

"The one thing these religions have in common is that they were all drummed up well before scientific discovery began." Peter sat in an armchair across from Taylor. "I realize that the last few days have been quite a whirlwind for you, and that you've probably been trying to determine exactly what has happened to you, and whether you can trust me. But I'm here to tell you that the only person you need to trust is yourself. If you do, the Program will bring you more reward than any religion ever could. Certainly more than any movie career could."

Taylor studied Peter's angular face. His skin glowed with the kind of taut sheen that could only have been achieved through surgery. "You're right," she lied. "I have to admit, I don't disagree with anything you've just said."

"That's because you're an actor. All great actors understand that the foundation of any great performance is letting yourself trust. Acting is a give-and-take dynamic. It requires a tremendous amount of comfort and trust in those you're working with, in the material given to you, and in the character you're playing. Wouldn't you agree?"

"I do," she said. "Actually, my first ever acting coach used to say the same thing. We spent the first week focused only on trust exercises. Falling backward into someone's arms, sharing an embarrassing secret with another student, walking blindfolded down a sidewalk with only someone's voice as a guide. I know what you're saying."

"So then you have unlocked the secret."

"I don't know if I would go that far, but I'm definitely committed to always trying to be a better actor."

"Some say the only actors who listen are the ones who are heard. A good actor listens to himself, to his co-performers, to his heart, to his teacher. Same goes for life. A fulfilled life is just the end result of a dedication to listening."

"How do you know so much about acting?"

Peter grinned. "Just between us?"

"Sure."

"It's not something I go and tell my patients. But I was once a child actor. A long, long time ago."

"Wow, and now you're a doctor. Impressive."

"Let's just say it's been quite an interesting journey."

"I'm sorry, but how old are you?"

"Old enough to know that I could be your father, who, by the way, could have used the Program."

"What do you mean?" Taylor asked.

Peter sighed. "I've been told your father died from skin cancer. Is that correct?"

"Yes, unfortunately, he did."

"Number four," Peter said, pointing at the list on the table in front of her.

Taylor gulped. "So this isn't a rehab. This is an anti-aging center?"

"Oh, Kensington is far more than that. Kensington is about tapping into and expanding human potential by following a very simple set of rules. Anti-aging is an utterly simplistic description of our mission. Before you complete your stay here you will learn all this. In due time."

Peter cleared his throat. "By the way, I spoke to your mother on the phone yesterday. I can see where you get your logical side from. She had a lot of questions, but she understood everything."

"Is she coming to get me?"

"She expressed some guilt for not being more in touch with you in the last couple years, for not being there for you. She just wants you to get well, which is why she's okay with you being under our care and conservatorship. It seems that she had no idea about your addiction struggle."

"Apparently neither did I," Taylor said.

Peter laughed. "The mind is a mysterious organ, far more than any other. And it can convince itself of just about anything. As such, if you are convinced that the Program will save you from the self-destructive part of your brain, then it will. Forever."

"That sounds like a long time. I have to say, I'm more of an in-the-moment kind of girl." Taylor yawned.

"The Program consists of the Work. And the Work demands a strict schedule. The body craves regularity. Your body secretes hormones when it is tired or stressed, when it is shocked by irregularity. It's close to bedtime. Why don't we let you rest and get back to Work tomorrow?"

"Okay. But for the record, you still didn't answer my original question."

"I'm sorry, what was it?"

"Your age? It's not a big deal. You can tell me. Age is just a number."

"I'm old enough to know that age is not just a number. I'm old enough to know that age *does* matter, numbers matter. Everything is numbered in our lives. The moment we are born we are given a birth date. Then a social security number is assigned to us so that we can be identified by the government. This numerical identity is inputted into a system of computers programmed with nothing more than a series of zeroes and ones coded together. From the time we can speak, we are asked, 'How old are you?' Then we go through life, each stage marked by reaching a certain age. Bar mitzvahs at thirteen. Voting at eighteen. Purchasing alcohol at twenty-one."

"I know that it matters. I was just saying it's not necessarily a bad thing, getting old."

"Go ahead and tell that to all the child stars who, the moment they hit puberty, are discarded into the show business trash bin! Tell that to the middle-aged actresses who can't get work because they are no longer the sexy ingénues they once were!"

Peter pounded his fist on the table as spit sprayed from his mouth. "Age is everything, you young dolt! You are sixteen.

They call it 'sweet sixteen.' But in my eyes, you are one year older than the perfect age—socially, sexually, intellectually. Ah, fifteen. If you could be forever fifteen, you would realize every fantasy of every religion in the world. You could live forever."

Taylor didn't know whether to admire him for his idealism or run from his creepy obsession.

"So, to answer your question," Peter said, turning calmer. "I am forty-five."

He tugged down at the sleeves of his linen sport coat and wiped a drop of spittle from his lip. "Age matters only when we give it the power to define us, kill us. The Program takes that power away. And you, Taylor, are the one who has been chosen to spread the gospel. You can save people."

"Why me?"

"Have you ever seen the play *Peter Pan*?" Peter asked.

"I've seen the movie."

"Then you might remember what Peter told Wendy."

Taylor hunched her shoulders as he walked behind her, placed a hand on the top of her head, and whispered, "One girl is worth more use than twenty boys."

A beater. That's what Tamara called her 2005 Toyota Corolla with 125,000 miles that chugged down the freeway, grayish exhaust spewing from the tail pipe.

Tamara's car had gotten Brooklyn all the way to the edge of the San Fernando Valley when Simone texted her.

> How close r u?

> > 20–30 mins . . . traffic sux!

> hurry up . . . i cant stay here too long, not safe here

Brooklyn put the phone down between her thighs. "Simone's getting antsy," she said.

"So who is this chick anyway?" Tamara asked.

"A source. She wants to show me something."

"And you promise that she can hook me up with an agent or somebody? The world needs to know the"—she lowered her voice like a baritone radio announcer—"one and only Tamaraaaa Curtiiiiis!"

"You know, you're not so bad for a bad influence," Brooklyn said.

"Who said I was a bad influence?"

"My mom."

Tamara shrugged. "I get it. She's a lawyer. She sees bad bitches whose lives in some ways look a lot like mine. At least she cares about you. My mom is more checked out than *Hunger Games* at the school library."

Brooklyn exploded into giggles. "Oh my god. I think I just peed myself."

"How many times do I have to tell you to wear a diaper around me?"

Tamara turned off on the exit for Nichols Canyon and headed up a hilltop. "By the way, I get why your mom thinks I am the Antichrist, but why's Holden so douchey to me?"

"He's just protective," Brooklyn said.

"Of what?"

"Me."

"Yeah, yeah, yeah," Tamara grumbled. "I'm the bad girl, the girl who swears, who dresses like a whore and gets kicked out of school. I'm such a baaaaad influence. Blah, blah, blah."

"Something like that, yes."

"Everyone needs a devil," Tamara said. "Even serial killers. 'Oh, the devil made me do it!'"

"Holden just wants me to be safe."

"If he's so protective, why didn't *he* drive you down here to meet with your sketch source?"

"Because he didn't want to get in trouble." Brooklyn didn't mention that Holden had already texted her three times in the last hour to make sure she was okay. It would just make Tamara think he was even more of a control freak. "He's just very conservative. It's his upbringing."

"If you ask me, that boy has balls the size of Tic Tacs."

"C'mon, his parents are just hardcore and put a lot of pressure on him to be perfect."

"I'm not talking about how he is with his parents. I'm talking about how he is around you. He is obviously still in love with you but too afraid to tell you. You guys have more sexual tension than those blood-suckers in those movies."

"Twilight?" Before Tamara could answer, Brooklyn pointed ahead to their right. "There!"

Tamara banked sharp at a private driveway flanked by tall palms and flicked on the high beams as she steered up to a black iron gate, which automatically swung open. A sleek, modern mansion loomed ahead.

As they pulled up to the house, Simone stepped out the front door to greet them.

Simone's usually stylish hair lay tangled, and dark circles rimmed her eyes as if she hadn't slept since she had last seen Brooklyn up in Twin Oaks.

"This is Tamara," Brooklyn said. "She's cool, don't worry."

Tamara shook Simone's hand hard. "Brookie's right. I only bite when I'm hungry."

"Fine, but you can't park the car here," Simone snapped. "And you can't be here. Just pull out and drive around the block, okay?"

Tamara glanced skeptically at Brooklyn. "I don't think so."

"Just trust me," Simone said. "It's safer this way."

"Brooklyn?" Tamara tilted her head. "You sure about this?"

"Yeah," she replied. "It's okay. I'll text you when we're done."

Tamara shrugged. "Fine." She climbed back in her car and drove out the gate.

Simone motioned to Brooklyn. "Come with me. The security monitor is in the pantry."

Simone allowed Brooklyn to step first through the silver front door, then she slammed it closed behind them. "Not too shabby, eh?" Simone said. "Taylor loves to sit out on the deck and watch the sunset. It's her favorite thing about the house."

"I've seen it in aerial pics, but never the inside." Brooklyn eyed the shiny white marble walls and high ceilings. The house wasn't flashy or pretentious, but it was still stunningly grand.

"Try decorating this monstrosity. I spent a year chasing down furniture to fill it."

Simone guided Brooklyn through the living room, into the kitchen, and finally to the spacious pantry. Shelves of food and drinks filled the left side like a mini grocery store. On the right sat a desk and chair. Simone pointed at the screen mounted on the wall above the desk. "There's the surveillance system."

Brooklyn could see on the black-and-white monitor a fuzzy image of Tamara reading her phone on the hood of her car.

Simone flicked a switch on a box connected to the monitor. "This house is actually twenty years old, and so is the surveillance system, if you can call it a system. Taylor never upgraded it. So it's basically just one camera fixed on the driveway. It's so old school that it records on a tape, but a really long-ass one, luckily."

Simone pressed Rewind, scanning the tape back to last Friday night. A minute or so later, she paused the tape and tapped the screen, pointing to the time code. "See? Those cops pulled up at 11:58 p.m."

Brooklyn leaned in close enough to make out a black SUV pulling into the driveway. Two beefy dudes carrying guns stepped out wearing dark clothes, but nothing resembling police uniforms. One held a white megaphone.

"This is strange." Brooklyn watched the men walk off camera to the side yard. "Is this all you got of them?"

"No." Simone fast-forwarded the tape. "Then there's this."

The video showed the two men returning to the SUV. One was carrying Taylor's limp body like a baby, her high-heeled feet dangling as he placed her into the backseat.

"Those aren't cops," Brooklyn said.

After putting Taylor in the car, the video showed one man climb in the back. The other guy closed the door, and as he walked around the back of the SUV, a younger guy in a T-shirt ran into frame, appearing to yell at the driver as he opened the back door and turned toward the camera.

Simone pressed Pause. "That's the Pretty Boy I told you about," she said. "See him?"

Despite the somewhat grainy resolution, Brooklyn could

still make out his chiseled face. "Oh my god, he *was* totally in on it." Brooklyn steadied her cell phone close to the screen and snapped a picture, which she immediately texted to Holden.

> remember the pic of the dude from the party I sent u? he's sketch. Look at this video still. we really must ID this guy. PS sorry for being such a bitch

Simone played the rest of the tape, which showed the SUV pulling out at 12:04 a.m. The resolution was too dark to make out a license plate number. Brooklyn snapped a pic of the car anyway, forwarding that to Holden as well.

"You were right, Simone," she said, pressing Send. "That's definitely a smoking gun."

Simone shrieked.

Then Brooklyn heard a male voice say, "Don't move!"

Brooklyn dropped her phone to the floor and threw her hands in front of her face. She felt a sharp stabbing pain in the nape of her neck and winced.

The man pushed her face down onto the desk. "I said, 'Don't move!'"

Then he swung Brooklyn around, forcing her to sit in the chair with one hand while tightly gripping a pistol in the other. Brooklyn looked up.

Pretty Boy.

The barrel shaking, he pointed the gun at her forehead. "You've made a very big mistake."

Brooklyn could see Simone sprawled face down on the tile floor just behind Pretty Boy, surrounded by a mess of fallen cans and bottles. A patch of blood was growing on the back of her head.

"I wouldn't shoot me if I were you," Brooklyn said.

"Oh, really. Why's that?"

"Because you'll get caught."

"I'm good at not getting caught. Unlike you."

Brooklyn stared into the barrel of the gun, hoping Simone was just unconscious.

"Who the hell are *you*?" he asked.

"Brooklyn Brant. I'm a reporter."

His eyes popped wide and his aim lowered toward the floor. "A reporter?"

"An investigative blogger. I cover celebrities."

Brooklyn could see sweat beading on his forehead. He pointed the pistol back at her. "What the hell are you doing here? You've made a big mistake, Red."

"I'm investigating the disappearance of Taylor Prince." She stared coldly into his eyes, which looked less dreamy and more panicky now. She pointed with her head to the monitor behind her. "I came to see that video."

His focus switched over to the video screen showing his image in freeze frame. He kept the gun aimed on her face.

Brooklyn didn't dare show her nerves. *A scared cop is a dead cop.* "You don't want to shoot me. It will only make things worse for you. And things are bad enough, my friend."

"What are you talking about?" he said, refocusing on Brooklyn.

"I already sent some screenshots of you to my assistant. And like it or not, he will have you ID'd within the hour."

"You're lying."

Simone groaned from the floor. *She's not dead.*

"In the corner," Pretty Boy barked, pointing to the far end of the pantry with his pistol. "And shut up."

"Have you ever heard of *false imprisonment*?" Brooklyn asked, stepping backward from him with her hands up.

He looked confused, making Brooklyn realize that while he may have been pretty, he wasn't the brightest bulb in the box.

"Just sit," he said.

Brooklyn knelt on the floor and began counting fours.

Four soup cans. Four foot taps. Four bananas. Four shelves. 1, 2, 3, 4 . . .

And praying.

Our Father, who art in heaven, hallowed be thy name. Thy kingdom come, thy will be done . . .

"By the way, holding a hostage is an automatic eight-year sentence," Brooklyn said. "Eight years."

Four goes into eight twice.

"Make that sixteen," she added.

Four times four is sixteen.

"When you count both me and her. That's two counts."

Pretty Boy reached under Simone's armpit and dragged her across the pantry, placing her head in Brooklyn's lap. The spot of blood on Simone's head had stopped spreading.

"Nobody's being held hostage," he said.

"Well, then there's always assault with a deadly weapon."

Pretty Boy stuffed the pistol in between his hip and the waist of his jeans. Combing his fingers through his wet hair, he paced the pantry. "She fell into the shelf and that can fell on her head. I didn't lay a hand on her."

He lifted a paper towel roll from the top shelf and tossed it to Brooklyn, who tore off a sheet, folded it, and began dabbing Simone's head wound.

"This is not good," he said. "*So* not good."

As he nervously jabbered on, Brooklyn counted his jittery steps.

"This gun doesn't even have bullets."

1 . . .

"I never meant to hurt anybody."

2 . . .

"I came here to make things right."

3 . . .

"He made me do it."

4 . . .

"Who made you do what?" Brooklyn asked. "God is the only one who has the power to make someone do something."

He dropped down into the chair. "So does the devil."

"Devil?" Brooklyn asked.

"My boss. That's what I call him." He glanced at the security monitor. "He's the person you want, not me."

Maybe Tamara was right: Everyone needs a devil to blame.

Cameras everywhere. Taylor had grown used to being watched. The paparazzi had become a daily reality she had accepted as yet another price of fame. But the fish-eye lenses stuck to the ceilings throughout Kensington felt more invasive than even the paps.

Taylor lay in bed listening to the dogs barking back at the howling desert coyotes. She had never believed what Peter and the staff claimed—that she was a danger to herself—but after a few days in treatment she felt like it could be true.

This would be a good place in which to lose one's mind, to drive someone to do something very self-destructive, to make them want to just tie that bed sheet around their neck . . .

Taylor slid out from the bed and walked barefoot over to the thick glass window, the palm trees holding watch like the guards outside her room and the dogs roaming the grounds.

Escape. The thought of it consumed her. But she knew that the only way she would gain freedom was by accepting their rules . . . acting the role. Suddenly, her door swung open. She jerked back upon seeing Peter, in a dark-green bathrobe, standing in the doorway holding a stack of clothes in his hand.

"Trouble sleeping?" he asked.

"A little."

He handed her a robe, then a two-piece black bikini.

"Put these on. It's time for a bath."

The phone. Distracted by her staring contest with the barrel of Pretty Boy's gun, Brooklyn had forgotten about the cell she had dropped. Until it rang.

Pretty Boy's eyes laser-locked on its location next to his feet. He picked it up and read the screen.

"Who's Tamara?" he asked.

"She's my ride," Brooklyn said. "She dropped me off. She's waiting outside for me. She's probably wondering if I'm okay. And I bet she's gonna call the cops unless she hears from me soon."

"Nah. She's heading home," Pretty Boy smirked.

"She wouldn't just leave. No way."

"She would if you told her to." He tapped out a message on the phone and showed Brooklyn the text exchange. "I'm sorry, Brooklyn Brant. But no one is leaving here until we are all on the same page."

He scrolled through more of her text messages. "And who's Holden?"

"That's my assistant I told you about."

"Looks like you're more than co-workers." He laughed. "He just texted that he loves you."

"Well, yeah, but that's none of your business. What is your business is that he has your picture, is a whiz with computers, and he's about to find out who you are. Unless I tell him to stop."

"He won't find anything, Red."

"Oh yes, he will. Trust me, he's found people with a lot less—"

"No, he won't. Because I don't exist."

Brooklyn laughed.

"Why did you come into this house anyway?" Pretty Boy asked.

"To meet with sleepyhead over here." Brooklyn pointed to Simone, whose head still rested in Brooklyn's lap. "She said she found out who kidnapped Taylor Prince. And after seeing the video, it looks like you're the creep. So tell me: Where is she?"

"Looks can be deceiving, Red."

"Yeah, like even a good-looking guy like you can be a total sociopath."

"I'm just the delivery man. I mean, what if I was just told to go pick up a package and bring it to them? A delivery guy doesn't know what someone does when they drop it off or where it goes from the drop-off point."

Brooklyn wished he weren't so attractive, because then it would be a lot easier to hate him. "You're obviously more than a delivery guy. You seem pretty tight with those mall cops in the security video."

"Let's say for the sake of argument that I did know where she was. How much would that information be worth to you?"

"Even if I had the money, I don't pay my sources. That's just dirty and unethical."

He laughed. "Then why would I tell anything to some kid with a blog who has no money? You get your story and I get nothing."

"You'd get peace of mind," she said.

"Peace is not possible for me until I'm free from him."

"From your boss?"

"Yes."

"Rule eleven . . ." Peter sat beside Taylor in the backseat as the SUV sped down the cactus-lined highway. "It states, 'I will drink 64 ounces of water a day and take mineral baths.'"

"So this is like a baptism?" she asked as the security guard parked at the edge of a white pebble beach.

"A baptism," Peter said, "is a silly religious ritual. This will be a medicinal bath. Since this lake has a very high salinity level, it offers many anti-aging and healing benefits."

Taylor followed Peter out of the vehicle. An orange glow shimmered off the expanse of water spread across the desert landscape in front of them.

Peter looked back at the guard. "Could we have some privacy?"

"Whatever you'd like, doctor," he said.

"We'll be back in a bit."

Her sandals crunching on the gravelly sand, Taylor followed Peter's shifting steps some fifty yards across the desolate beach to the water's edge. Another crunch. She stopped and looked down to find a dried-out fish skeleton under her foot.

"Gross!" She one-hopped away, dodging the dozens of other dead fish she now realized lay scattered on the beach.

"You're safe," Peter assured her. "A couple of years ago, the oxygen levels in the water got too low, partly because of a spike in salinity. There was a massive fish die-off." He picked up one of the dehydrated corpses and squeezed it between his hands. It crumbled into powder. Peter smiled. "It's just nature."

The anxiety that twisted Taylor's stomach from being alone with Peter in a fish graveyard was at least somewhat canceled out by the freedom she felt. It was the first time she had left the Kensington compound.

"Shall we?" he asked.

"Okay," she shrugged.

Peter untied his robe and slid out to reveal tight-fitting exercise shorts. A wave of relief came over Taylor. *He's not naked.*

As he stepped into the water, she tried not to stare at his pale, scrawny body, but she couldn't help it.

"Don't be shy," he said.

When Taylor disrobed, Peter's eyes brightened.

Though the summer air felt hot and dry on her skin, Taylor crossed her arms in front of her chest to shield herself from his icy gaze.

"Take a soak," he said, falling backward with a splash, laughing like a child.

Taylor dipped her right foot in, surprised at its warmth. "It's actually hot," she said.

"Just about ninety degrees this time of year."

Taylor stepped in until she was waist deep and squatted down, letting the water envelop her shoulders. A splash came up into her mouth. "Blech," she spat. "So salty."

Peter lapped the water over his blemish-free skin and rubbed his hands over his face. "About twice as salty as the Pacific. And a lot warmer." He waded an arm's length from Taylor. "Back in the day, they used to call this the 'Hollywood Riviera.' Celebrities like the Marx Brothers kept their yachts here. It was a celebrity playground."

"Then what happened?"

"They abandoned it, went on to the next thing." His expression turned from gleeful to forlorn. "Hollywood has always been obsessed with the *new* thing."

Peter looked up at the stars that just began twinkling in the twilight, then at Taylor. "Do you ever worry about that happening?"

"What?"

"Being abandoned when you're no longer young, no longer the new thing?"

"I've thought about it. Just the nature of the business, of life really."

"But it doesn't have to be, you see? That's why you're here. With me." He floated on his back. "Darwin had it right. We must always evolve. We can change things."

In any other scenario, watching a man floating faceup in a warm bath of natural salt water on a starry summer night might have been the stuff of romance. But instead, it inspired much darker visions in Taylor's mind. After all, Peter was short, with hardly any muscle on his bones.

I could kill him.

Taylor stared skyward and saw it clearly playing out like it might in one of her movies. Hit him on the head with a rock, then hold him underwater until he stops breathing. She could swim off into the darkness, across the shore and get help. Escape.

"I said, 'Let's go!'"

Startled, Taylor stood in the water. Peter was already on the shore in his robe. "It's getting late."

Taylor wrung her hair dry. Her attack would have to wait.

When they got back in the car for the ten-minute drive back to the compound, Taylor flexed her acting muscles.

"Thank you, Peter. Tonight was magical. And, well, thank you for saving my life."

Peter flashed a self-satisfied glance at his grateful disciple.

"I'm sorry," Brooklyn said. "But I don't even know your name."

"Nice try, Red," Pretty Boy replied. "You're very clever. But I'm not telling you anything more until I hear more from you. We need to have an understanding, an agreement. I don't know if I can trust you."

"You can," she said.

"If I let you go, what's to stop you from leaving here and telling the cops?"

"Well, I haven't yet."

"That's because I have your phone."

"But I've had this one." She pulled her right hand out from behind Simone's back to reveal Simone's phone.

"Then why didn't you call the cops?"

"Maybe I didn't call the cops because I had a hunch that you aren't a bad person, just maybe a good person who's made bad choices."

Pretty Boy slid the gun across the floor to her feet. "It's a toy. I never meant to hurt anybody."

Brooklyn picked up the gun and inspected it. Indeed, it was made of light plastic.

"All I want is a fresh start," he added.

"Are you religious?"

"Not really. Why?"

"Because I am. I'm Catholic."

"And?"

"Religious or not, you would probably agree with me that the truth shall set you free," Brooklyn said, paraphrasing her favorite verse, John 8:32.

"Easy for you to say. The truth will get you the story, but it could also get me killed."

"Look. I don't know what you're talking about exactly, but whatever your situation, it also might set you free."

Pretty Boy exhaled. "So. This blog of yours."

"Deadline Diaries."

"Yeah. Let's say I told you where Taylor was, who was keeping her, and what she was doing in there. Would you run that story?"

"If it were true, yes. Of course I would have to verify it with at least another source first."

"But no one would ever know I told you." He pointed at Simone. "Not even her."

"Of course not. But you better talk fast because she's been out a while and is about to come to."

"Okay," Pretty Boy said. "How do I know for sure that you won't tell anyone?"

"You would have to trust me."

"I'm not good at trust."

"I have a really strong belief that nothing amazing or important in this world has ever happened between two people without trust," Brooklyn said. "Without trust between two lovers, there would be no true love, no genuine marriage, no sacred bond. Without trust between a kid and their parents, a kid would feel unprotected and uncared for. Without trust between governments, there would be no peace. Without trusting a pilot to do his job, no one would ever get on a freaking plane. And no one would ever have surgery if they didn't trust a doctor to do their job and not kill them. So what I'm saying is that without trust, no journalist could ever break a big story."

Pretty Boy paced the pantry. Simone stirred with a moan. "I've spent my whole life wanting to trust people. I wanted to trust my mom when she bailed on me and sent me to live with my crack-head uncle in ninth grade. Then I wanted to trust my uncle when he got me hooked on meth and forced me into hustling, selling my body to old guys so we could both get high."

"I'm sorry," Brooklyn said. "I had no idea."

"And I wanted to trust my boss when he got me out of jail and promised to give me a clean slate. But he lied, Brooklyn. Instead, all he has done is blackmailed me and forced me to do his dirty work."

"Such as?"

"Deliver him his so-called packages."

"But you can stop this. If I report your boss and reveal just how evil he is, you can stop him. Then you can be free."

"You don't understand. Everyone believes him. He has power over so many people. Cops, politicians, Hollywood managers and agents. He also controls the media. My boss plants stories on *STARSTALK* all the time. He has the power to have me put back in prison. He is always saying that without him, prison would be my Forever Land."

"That's a tad dramatic, don't you think? I mean, who is this guy?"

"I call him Dr. Evil," he replied. "Look, he came to me when I was at the lowest point of my life. I had just been arrested for my third violent felony and faced life in prison for it. I was only nineteen. So he came into the county jail one day and promised he could make the old me disappear, get me totally off the grid and into hiding. But with one hitch. I would have to work for him. Of course I did. I had no other option, and I *trusted* him. He paid off the cops, arranged to have my identity changed and my criminal record cleared. But for the last two years, he has held that power over me."

"But now you can turn the tables on him," Brooklyn said.

"Yeah, right." He laughed.

"People only believe lies, no matter how big, when they don't know the truth," said Brooklyn. "As a matter of fact, in the absence of truth, people will believe any lie, no matter how big. So tell me, where is she?"

"I can tell you where Taylor is," Pretty Boy said. "But the bigger story is about where almost every major young celebrity over the last ten years has gone when they have supposedly suffered from an addiction or an eating disorder or dehydration or exhaustion or a nervous breakdown. Even depression or getting arrested for assault or drug possession. And Brooklyn, what could happen next to Taylor is even bigger."

Brooklyn stood up and carefully stepped toward him. "I will not reveal your identity. Not to police, not to my readers, not to anyone, including this boss of yours. You have my word." Stopping an arm's reach from him, she extended her right hand. "Shake?"

Pretty Boy's large hand enveloped hers as he shook it. "My name is Beckett."

"Nice to meet you, Beckett."

"I will tell you everything, but . . ." Beckett glanced at Simone groaning back to consciousness. "But first I have to go pay a visit out in the desert. I have some unfinished business with him."

Beckett handed Brooklyn back her phone. "Now that I have your number, I'll text you tomorrow."

Please, God. Give me strength. Then came nine rings—the brass bell from atop Casa Bell signaling it was Rest Time.

The nurse entered Taylor's room as if on cue. "You need to get your rest. Trouble sleeping?"

"Yes."

"Try these." The nurse handed Taylor two large white pills. "It's melatonin, an herb. It will help regulate your sleep."

"Thank you." Taylor sat back onto the mattress and dropped the pills into her mouth, washing them down with water from the cup on her nightstand. "What's your name?"

"Mary."

"And your last name?"

"Darling," the nurse whispered. "Mary Darling. But we aren't supposed to share our last names with patients."

"Our little secret," Taylor whispered back with a wink.

Nurse Mary looked away and reached for the curtains. She snapped them shut. "Tomorrow is a big day. Visitor's Day."

"Who's visiting?" Taylor asked.

"That I don't know. Only Dr. Kensington knows."

Taylor reached for the nurse's hand and squeezed it. "Am I going to be okay?"

Nurse Mary squeezed back. "Yes, you will. But you must do as Dr. Kensington tells you, Ms. Prince."

Taylor sat up. "What happens to people who don't finish the Program?"

The nurse shook her head. "Dr. Kensington believes failure is not an option. I've been here since Kensington opened eleven years ago. I have seen a lot of young stars like you, with varying results. My best advice, Ms. Prince, is to just focus on the Work." She patted Taylor on the wrist. "Dr. Kensington likes to say, 'Nothing is really work unless you would rather be doing something else.' My advice is to not want to do anything else."

"Are you afraid of him, too?" Taylor whispered.

Mary pulled her hand away.

"Has he hurt you?"

Mary locked eyes with her young patient.

"What's he going to do to me?"

Mary rolled her eyes up toward the security camera and back down to Taylor.

"I understand," Taylor said. "Thank you, nurse. Good night."

WEDNESDAY, AUGUST 6 | 🕐 9:02 PM

Nichols Canyon Road • LOS ANGELES, CA

"Wakey, wakey. Eggs and bakey!" Brooklyn said.

Simone's eyes blinked open. "What the . . . What happened?" She sat up on the couch, pushing away the ice pack that Brooklyn had been holding on her forehead.

"Dude, a ginormous can of soup fell on your head and it knocked you out. You've been in and out for the last few minutes. You don't remember anything?"

"Not really," Simone groaned.

"You had me worried there for a while."

Brooklyn didn't mention the bomb of information that Beckett dropped while Simone lay in her stupor. Nor did she mention how Beckett had carried Simone from the pantry to the couch, leaving a minute before she fully came to. Brooklyn didn't consider not sharing all the information a violation of the ninth commandment. It wasn't *technically* a lie. And she had promised Beckett total anonymity.

"I sort of remember showing you the security footage, but it's all foggy, to be honest," Simone said.

"Yeah. You showed me those guys with the guns. And I saw Pretty Boy on the tape, too. You have helped a lot. I think just having that footage is enough to start back-reporting."

"Back *what*?"

"Back-reporting is when you go backward to figure out the story. Like I will start with trying to identify those guys, and from there figure out who they are, why they were there, why they took Taylor away, and ultimately, where Taylor is now."

Brooklyn placed the ice pack next to Simone on the couch.

"As for you, sleepyhead, you just need to relax here for a while. I gotta get back to Twin Oaks, hopefully before midnight.

Tamara's waiting outside for me." She handed Simone two Advils from her purse. "Take these and get some rest. I'll text you tomorrow."

Simone took the tiny pills. "Thanks. But what about Pretty Boy?"

"I'm on it. I emailed Holden some screen grabs from the footage, and he is already back home researching. I'm going to track down Taylor, don't worry. We had a breakthrough tonight. We are much closer to finding her. Much, much closer."

"I want to help."

"You already have," Brooklyn said. "And I will need more of your help. I have a plan."

"What is it?"

Brooklyn smirked and love-tapped Simone on the cheek four times. "Let's just say that as soon as I find out where she is, we're all going on a little field trip."

Feeling like she simultaneously survived a near-death experience and won the lottery all within the last hour, Brooklyn stepped down the driveway and out the gate, where Tamara waited in her car.

The moment Brooklyn landed in the passenger's seat, Tamara snapped, "Why did you tell me to go home, then tell me to come right back, then just go totally MIA? I was already halfway back to Twin Oaks, you little ginger queen!"

"I'm so sorry. Things got weird."

Tamara pulled a U-turn and drove down the winding canyon road toward the 101. "I'm just glad you're okay. Can't have bitches dying on me. Especially you. Your mom already thinks I am the Great Satan."

A few minutes up the freeway, the radio blaring KIIS-FM pop, Brooklyn reached to the control panel and turned down the volume.

"Tamara, do you think I'm crazy?" Brooklyn asked.

"Duh, yeah. Now turn the radio back up."

"No, I'm being serious. Do you think I am mental?"

Tamara kept her eyes on the road. "We're all mental, Brooklyn. It's part of being human. We all just have different issues."

"What's yours?"

"I think mine are rather obvious."

"That you're the funniest person I know?"

"Honestly, that's my issue. I need to make people laugh because I want everyone to be happy. I want to be a comedian, but comedians aren't born. They're made. Do you even know why I started telling jokes?"

"Because you like to make people laugh?"

"No. Well, yeah, but more of what started it was my parents fighting all the time. They would argue over the dumbest crap, constantly. So when I was a kid, I would tell jokes to make them laugh, hoping they would just shut up and get along."

"You were a laugh doctor," Brooklyn said.

"More like a scared kid trying to make peace."

"Well, you helped me. When my dad died, you were the only person in the neighborhood who didn't walk on eggshells around me. Everyone was like, 'Oh, poor, Brooklyn Brant.' They would either talk to me like a baby or just avoid me all together. But do you remember what you said to me at his funeral?"

Eyes glued on the road ahead, Tamara nodded.

Brooklyn swallowed back the lump in her throat. "You said, 'Hey, your dad's lucky. He didn't have to listen to that priest for the last hour.'"

"So inappropriate."

"Death is inappropriate. Police coming to your house in the middle of the night to tell you and your mom that your father is dead is inappropriate. Never finding his body is inappropriate. Never finding out what happened to him is inappropriate. Not sharing everything they knew about the circumstances of his death is inappropriate. But cracking a joke to make a twelve-year-old kid feel better? *That* was appropriate. It was healing."

"I have a whole philosophy about that," Tamara said.

"About my boogers bubbling out of my nose when I cry?"

"No, I'm being serious. People do different things to heal themselves, to help them cope with life. It's like a survival instinct. I make people laugh so that I don't feel so sad. A writer might tell a story to gain a greater understanding of a problem that bothers them. Some pray. A lot of singers want to perform so they can escape their own sad reality. You do the same, Brant."

"I'm definitely not a singer. There goes that theory."

"No, but you're a reporter. By finding stuff out, you're healing that part of you that hurts because you never found out what exactly happened to your dad."

Brooklyn let the truth of Tamara's observation soak in to the whir of the tires on the freeway pavement.

"Pretty wise stuff from a seventeen-year-old dropout comedian," Brooklyn said.

"I might be school stupid, but I'm life smart. And don't believe it when someone says age is only a number, because that's not true. We are students in the school of life, and time is the greatest teacher of them all."

Thirty minutes. That's how long Kensington members could spend in the garden with an "approved" visitor once a week.

Taylor had asked for Simone to visit. Peter claimed that Simone could not be located by any of his staff. Taylor had then requested her mother, but Peter explained her mother would only be allowed on "Family Day" on the last day of treatment, in three weeks. He promised her a "special visitor" instead.

Standing next to a rock-walled waterfall in the palm-shrouded garden outside the back of the center, Taylor sipped from her always-present bottle of coconut-infused mineral water, an intake carefully monitored for a daily dose of 64 ounces.

She had already completed the first six hours of her daily "rejuvenation regimen." She had woken, eaten her egg whites with avocado, and washed down her pack of vitamins and herbal pills with freshly squeezed orange juice from the grove on the Kensington grounds. She had applied her sunscreen before doing yoga, meditation, and breathing exercises. After an hour-long Delete Session with Helper Lily (in which Lily encouraged Taylor to "delete" the trauma of her father's death from her mind), she had gone to the study room to read twenty pages of her Program assignment, *Peter Pan*. However, Taylor hardly considered a childish fairy tale about a bunch of kids who didn't want to grow up the stuff of rejuvenation and recovery world-changing power.

Pebbles rustled on the garden path behind her. Taylor spun around to see a stunningly handsome guy walking toward her, with broad shoulders that tapered down to a narrow waist.

"Evan!" she squealed, running up to him and hugging him tightly.

She hadn't seen Evan Ryan in almost a month, when they had both attended a marketing meeting for the movie they had shot earlier in the year. He had appeared far more reserved than normal, and there had not been a smile to be seen on his normally grinning face. His publicist did most of the talking that day, with Evan speaking only a few times in what was almost a robotic mumble.

"How'd you find me?" she asked.

Evan gripped her shoulders. "Dr. Kensington invited me. He said he had a plan for us."

She leaned closer. "So you've met Peter?"

He looked nervously over his shoulder. "Yeah, Taylor. I know him well. He's my doctor."

"So what's his deal? Is he a legit doctor?"

"He's trying to help you. Like he helped me. And many others like us."

"So *this* is where you went away to rehab."

"Yes, but as you've probably come to realize, it's more like a school for living a healthy life than rehab. Honestly, Taylor, Dr. Kensington has not only saved my life, he is prolonging it."

Taylor studied Evan's face, noticing that as his mouth moved, the muscles around it stayed still, rendering him virtually expressionless. He seemed like a shell of the guy she had worked with. His entire demeanor resembled that of George and the other Kensington staffers.

"I don't understand, Evan. You seemed perfectly fine before you came here. No offense, but you've changed and you seem like you're stoned. Or brainwashed."

"I'm an actor, you must remember," he replied. "And trust me, I was hiding a lot—not just from you, but from a lot of people, including myself. This is who I am, this is my human potential realized. The person you knew before the Program was destined for a short, unhappy life. Dr. Kensington has unlocked the secret."

Taylor shook him by the shoulders. "Evan. What the hell are you talking about?"

"Secrets. I kept dark secrets. Even from myself. And I learned that these secrets can kill you if you don't deal with them—if you don't share them."

"Evan, everyone keeps secrets. As a matter of fact, Dr. Kensington insists that I can't tell anyone I've been treated here. You call that treatment? I call that hypocrisy—and lunacy."

"Some secrets are dark. They eat at you a little bit, a day at a time. They create stress, anxiety, fears. All this pressure can take years off your life. The Program gives you a safe place to share everything, to bring you into the moment and onto the Path. Our practice is a secret worth keeping."

Taylor stared into his vacant eyes. She wanted to knock some sense of reality into him. But the rehearsed way he talked made her worry that he no longer was on her side. Convincing him to change his mind was futile.

Just act.

"You called it a path," she said. "To where?"

"The path to Forever Land."

"Huh?"

"He hasn't told you about Forever Land?"

"No. What are you talking about, Ev?"

"Here's the deal," he whispered. "If you successfully complete the Program, then he lets you into Forever Land."

"So is that where you have been?"

Evan laughed. "It's not a place; it's a state of being."

"OK, fine. So have you been there?"

"Not yet. I have just one more project to complete. Some video project. But I'm the first recruit." He lifted his left pant leg and revealed a black tattoo on his back ankle:

$$\infty \atop 1$$

He rubbed his fingers over it. "Infinity. Forever."

"And I'm the second?" She turned to show him her matching infinity tattoo:

$$\infty \atop 2$$

"Yes, and when we pass all our tests, we get into Forever Land for life."

Taylor reached up to tug at her hair in frustration. When her fingertips slid off her bare head, she remembered none existed.

"So tell me, what happens in this place that is not an actual place?" she asked. "What can you do there that you can't do anywhere else?"

"From what I've been told by everyone here, it's a place where you never have to grow up, where you never get old, where things like disease and death are the exception rather than the rule. It's a place where you can stay forever fifteen."

"Sounds like someone has a *Peter Pan* obsession and has taken it way too far."

"It's more than that."

"C'mon, why would someone want to stay fifteen forever? There's the acne, for starters. And maybe it's not a problem for you, but my hormones can make me act like a crazy person. I'm fine with leaving fifteen behind." Taylor fashioned finger quotes, adding, "Forever."

"I don't think he means you literally stay fifteen, but rather you retain all the benefits of being young," Evan said.

Taylor shook her head. "Sorry. I *want* to grow up. I'm looking forward to growing old and wrinkly and wise. I want to have my body change, my hips grow wider, the lines in my face deepen. I want to feel the aches of being old because that means I've lived, that I have experienced things that other people, younger people, have not. Aging is part of nature. Things grow old and die; new things are then born and go through the whole cycle again. We learned all about this basic biology stuff in third grade, Evan. I don't think it's smart to mess with nature. People once thought fossil fuels were totally awesome and harmless, but now they're destroying our planet."

"That's different," Evan shot back. "Those fifteen rules are actually good for you. They're not going to kill you."

"Yeah? Do you even know what's in those IV bags they're pumping into us?"

"Yeah. Vitamins, nutrients."

"That's what they claim, but you don't really know, do you?" Evan shook his head.

"And those injections, Evan. They *can* kill you."

"Well, I've never felt more energized, clean, and pure. And by the way, Vitamin B-12 can't kill you, Taylor."

"Those aren't vitamins in those vials."

"How do you know that?"

"It's human growth hormone," Taylor said quietly. "I saw it was HGH on one of the nurse's bottles. I've heard this stuff can give people tumors, heart problems, stuff like that. It's dangerous. Peter has lied to us. God knows what other lies he's telling us that we haven't found out yet."

Evan's eyes narrowed. Taylor sensed for the first time that she had possibly broken through his brainwashed barrier.

"Peter talks about this all being a fountain of youth," she continued. "But there's no such thing. Do you remember learning about Ponce de León?"

"Of course. The explorer?"

"Yeah, he sailed from Europe to Florida in search of the so-called 'Fountain of Youth.' The Native Americans had told him about a magical fountain where people could have their youth restored after drinking or bathing in its waters. But you know what? He never found it! No one did back then—or ever since. That's because there is *no such thing* as the Fountain of Youth. And I highly doubt if there was one, it would be found here in the middle of the bum-sucking desert!"

"Dr. Kensington is just trying to help us. He cares. He warned me you have been resisting the Program, that you were still carrying around traumas and in denial about your issues. Now I can see for myself that this is the case."

Taylor grabbed Evan by the arm. "You're not going to tell him anything I just said, are you?"

Evan shoved her hand back at her. "Rule number eight: 'I will delete my traumas with Staff and never lie to Staff.'"

Three days. It had been three days since Brooklyn's encounter with Beckett in the pantry. Before leaving the house, Beckett had promised he would text her the next day, but as of yet Brooklyn had heard nothing.

Holden's research had proved equally unproductive. Even he had not been able to get any closer to identifying the security guards. Brooklyn's own research into possible rehabs in Southern California didn't yield any breaks, either. And no leads or any hint of where Taylor could be had come from Twitter or Instagram.

Gnawing at her fingernails until the cuticles bled, Brooklyn had grown more agitated, more unable to focus on anything but the story. Brooklyn had gone to swim practice with Holden on Friday. She had also tried to read a book, but kept re-reading the first page over and over because she couldn't focus. Beckett held the key to unlocking the secret to Taylor's whereabouts, and Brooklyn kicked herself for not getting more information out of him when she had the chance. If Beckett flaked out, it would be the journalistic equivalent of a detective letting a serial killer go free after an interrogation without a confession. Disastrous.

Brooklyn felt she had no choice but to restore some order to the chaos. And it being Saturday night, she could engage in the ultimate ritual in her Fourmation playbook.

The brown-brick Cathedral of St. Francis stood on Main Street, next door to a Wells Fargo and across the street from the Twin Oaks Police headquarters. St. Francis was where Brooklyn had been baptized, where she had made her First Communion, and, just two years ago, where she had her Confirmation.

It was also where she had mourned her father's death four years ago in a ceremony fit for a fallen general.

Brooklyn walked up the stone front stairs in a long, white, ankle-length cotton skirt and canary top. Her mom had said this outfit made her look like an Easter egg—white, yellow, and red on top—but it remained Brooklyn's favorite.

On her father's funeral day, Brooklyn had dressed appropriately dark. Brooklyn remembered the white-gloved officers carrying her father's flag-draped coffin down the center aisle to the awaiting hearse, the touching remembrances of fellow cops, and of friends, and a homily from Father McGavin. The church had been standing-room-only that afternoon, with an overflow crowd in the lobby to pay their respects.

On this Saturday evening, however, the sanctuary echoed with near emptiness.

Brooklyn picked her favorite pew. She performed the sign of the cross and slid onto the bench, placing the kneeling pad down, closing her eyes, and folding her hands in silent prayer.

Hail Mary, full of grace, the Lord is with you . . .

Brooklyn believed that traditional prayers such as "Hail Mary" opened up the ears of the Holy Father, as well as departed spirits. So once the prayer was completed, Brooklyn began silently talking to her own father.

Dad, I miss you. But I feel your presence, and I know you are always there for me. Your spirit is always with me. I know you are watching me and I want to make you proud. Like you, my work is my mission to spread the values of truth and justice. But I am stuck. I fear that Taylor Prince could be in danger. I could use some divine inspiration or a sign or any guidance. I know you and God are very tight. So if you could please put in a good word for me, I will not let you down. In the name of the Father, the Son, and the Holy Spirit. Amen.

Brooklyn liked that each Catholic Mass was anchored with four parts: the Introductory Rites, the Liturgy of the Word, the Liturgy of the Eucharist, and the Concluding Rites. The physical act of performing the four-pointed sign of the cross offered her a calm like no other. Yet she questioned the authenticity of stories more than two thousand years old. She knew how slippery the truth could be and that there could be as many versions of events as there were people who witnessed them. But she didn't question the calming peace she found in the Mass, or her ability to communicate to God and her father. She hadn't lost faith.

"Today's reading is from the book of Revelation," announced Father McGavin from the pulpit. "Chapter one, verse eight. 'I am the Alpha and the Omega, who is and who was, and who is to come, the Almighty.' Alpha is the first letter of the Greek alphabet and Omega is the last. God is not only saying that he is the first and the last of everything, the one who can create and end life, but also that he is eternal. You need not look any farther than Him, for he is, what we in modern parlance might say, the end-all and be-all. We will find eternal life through faith in Him."

And then that's when Brooklyn experienced a revelation of her own. *Alpha and Omega.* An *A* and an *O*. Letters. The license plate.

Thank you, Dad.

"The Singularity," Dr. Kensington lectured his two disciples in his high-pitched voice. "The idea is to live long enough to experience what is known as the Singularity. That is the moment in human evolution where computer intelligence, our understanding of human biology, and our brain-computer technologies have developed to such a point that humans will possess a technological super-intelligence. At this stage, we'll be able to extend our lives indefinitely. That is why we must live healthfully, and we must follow the Program."

The gnome-ish doctor stood over Evan and Taylor in the garden, his hands buried in the pockets of his seersucker linen pants.

"Some scientists believe the Singularity could happen as soon as the 2020s. Others predict the year to be more like 2045. Either way, if we adopt the proper lifestyle, it could easily occur within our lifetimes. Once we hit the Singularity, and we have total control over our biology with computers and cyber-treatments, we will no longer live within biological boundaries. Illness will no longer exist, and, therefore, death will no longer exist.

"You see, we have identified segments of DNA that get shorter as a cells age. These segments are called telomeres. When enough telomeres die, a cell can't reproduce anymore and ultimately dies. When enough cells die, we die. But from the moment you enrolled in the Program, among the daily supplements you've taken has been a pill containing an enzyme called telomerase. It's scientifically proven that telomerase not only stops the cell death, it also reverses it. What I'm trying to tell you is that you have within you the building blocks for immortality."

Taylor raised her hand.

"Yes," Dr. Kensington said.

"Okay, so this enzyme reverses aging," Taylor said. "But what does this have to do with religion?"

The doctor stepped forward and held Taylor's face in his hands. "My child. The naïveté of your youth never ceases to endear you to me. Religion only exists because we have a fear of dying. Take away our fear, and we no longer need their supposed God. That, in a nutshell, is why they don't want this to exist. I'm a threat to their order. But it is my mission to save humanity, not the church. And this is the magic pill."

He took his hands off her. "But first we have some PR work to do."

Peter escorted Taylor and Evan across the main lawn to the living room of Casa Bell, where he handed them each a twenty-page bound document. "This," Peter said, "will inspire the masses to find the path to Forever Land."

Taylor held the document in both hands and read the cover page.

An Untitled Music Video Treatment
for "Forever Young"

Directed by
Dr. Peter Kensington

Starring
Evan Ryan (Peter) and Taylor Prince (Wendy)

Music by
Jason Wild

Lyrics by
Dr. Peter Kensington

"This music video will not only go viral, it will tell the greatest love story of your generation. It will inspire others to join the Program. This project is nothing short of your destiny, the end result of all the events that led you here. This, my friends, will mark the start of your professional comeback from your personal struggles," Peter told them.

"I'm honored, Dr. Kensington," Evan said. "And to bring Taylor and me together for this is absolutely genius casting. Not to mention what we both need to revive our careers. I am a hundred percent on board."

"Certainly, for two actors who have had to go to rehab in the same year, joining in a film project with themes such as the ones in this video will send a powerful message. And Jason Wild's song is nothing short of a musical masterpiece."

Peter adjusted the paisley square billowing from the chest pocket of his blazer. "This project will raise the bar. Hollywood has run out of interesting, compelling, game-changing narratives. It's all the same old formula, made by the same old studios, same old directors, and starring the same old actors. Combining a hit pop song with two of the greatest actors of the Forever Generation will inspire a whole new form of entertainment."

He held out his phone to his young disciples. "Take a listen."

The song was classic Jason Wild, with poetic lyrics set to a techno beat, straddling the fine line between cheesy and inspirational.

Wendy was a girl from the heartland
Turning sixteen soon, she was the lead singer of a band

Peter was older, longed to forever be a boy
Appeared in Wendy's life like a dream, to bring her the
    same childlike joy

Wendy didn't want to grow any older
Thought Peter represented a power that proved bolder

A youthful Neverland the two jumped above
Came fame, fortune, and ultimately a love

For all things fresh, forever, and true
Wendy sang a song for her guy, simply called "I love you"

I love the stars, love the moon, love the way you make
me swoon
Teach me to fly, I'll follow you high, singing together our
favorite tune

It's a belief that can only be sung
Lovers willing to die to achieve the state of being For-
ever Young

"Take a few days to read the treatment, learn your scenes, become one with your characters. Then we will shoot next Monday and Tuesday," Peter said.

Taylor looked at Evan, then back at Peter. "So soon?"

"Seeing as though we only have you here for less than two weeks now, we must use our time wisely."

Taylor asked, "Why is the project untitled?"

"I'll tell you why!" Peter shouted. "Because this project is a collaboration. This is not the old-school Hollywood. This is not where child stars are ordered to do something and have no say in what they're doing. Indeed, because this is a *collaboration*, you and Evan will title the project yourselves. Does this appeal to you, Taylor? Or would you rather spend your life being told what to do, being controlled and judged and kept down by Hollywood tyrants?"

"I, I—"

"Enough, Ms. Prince. You will only truly learn by doing. And you are doing this project."

After Evan left the house, Peter escorted Taylor to the upstairs study, leaving her alone to read the script. The study beat the antiseptic blandness of the clinic, though Taylor realized the disturbing subtext of the "punishment and reward" system that Peter had explained the other day.

Keek, keek, keek!

The sound of the squealing monkey rattling around in its cage echoed up the stairs to Taylor.

"Rafferty, down!" Peter barked from the floor below.

Taylor put the script down.

"I don't like animals," Taylor heard a familiar man's voice say. "Especially when they are screaming at me."

"It's not the animal, it's the cage, Beckett," Peter answered. "Rafferty really doesn't like being put in a cage. You can't blame Rafferty for not wanting to be put behind bars, can you?"

"No, sir," Beckett replied. "Can't blame him at all."

Taylor tiptoed from the couch to the doorway of the study, pressing her ear up to the door.

"Which brings me to your latest delivery," Peter said. "You probably came here wanting to get paid, didn't you?"

"Of course. That was our deal."

"I'm sorry, Beckett. I can't pay you today. I simply don't have a reward for you today."

"But I delivered you Taylor. That's who you wanted, isn't it? That was our deal."

"Yes, it was. But you failed to also deliver someone else. The assignment was to bring me Taylor and her assistant. But you let her get away. Simone was ripe for the picking. We need another recruiter. Now she has gone rogue. This is not good for you."

"I tried, but she wouldn't take the bait," Beckett said. "I made the moves on her, but she didn't seem to care. Taylor, however, I had wrapped around my pinkie. Just like you taught me."

Taylor realized then who was talking: Pretty Boy. She shook her head in disbelief that she had fallen for his deception.

"You are a beautiful young man, Beckett. That's partly why I hired you. But beauty can only get you so far."

"I tried, Dr. Kensington. I really did."

"I'm starting to get the feeling that you aren't hearing me correctly. It was a package deal—both Taylor and Simone. Since you failed to deliver the package, you don't get paid. Those are the rules."

Those evil bastards! Taylor clenched her jaw tightly to silence her breathy anger.

"I promised, but you also made me promises," Beckett shot back. "You promised me more than money. You promised me a new life for helping you bring these kids to you. You promised me freedom."

"You made promises, too, my son, and you broke them," Peter said. "What we have here is a simple breakdown in trust. And without trust, we can't work together."

"When we started this relationship, you wanted me to bring you adults who had addiction issues," Beckett said. "I felt like no matter how wrong on some levels, I was at least helping sick people. But then it became all about the kids—these teens who didn't even really have problems. This is not what I signed up for."

"Oh, but it is," Peter said. "I can show you the contract you signed that day in the jail."

"I don't care what you can show me. I can guarantee you that it says nothing about kidnapping, nothing about you brainwashing kids. Definitely nothing about shocking patients. Are you going to shock Taylor, too?" Beckett raised his voice, while Taylor muzzled herself with both hands to contain her mounting disgust—and fear. "Are you going to delete all of Taylor's memories? Are you going to ask me to tie her down and watch her foam at the mouth until her brain is so fried that she has no personality, let alone a memory? Evan didn't deserve that. Neither did Jason Wild."

"Electroshock therapy is a last resort. It's only used when—"

"When Jason Wild tells you to go screw yourself and write your own songs? Or when Evan refuses to cut ties with his parents?"

"Stop. I am warning you. Just stop. By the way, whatever happened to bringing me that blogger who's been snooping around and calling everyone? That *Deadline Diaries* girl."

"Brooklyn Brant? Oh, she never showed up at the house."

"Oh, okay. But you're lying."

Keek, keek, keek!

"I have a question for you, Beckett. What is my name?"

"Dr. Peter Kensington."

"So then why would you call me 'Dr. Evil'?"

"That's obviously just a joke."

"Am I laughing?" Peter asked. "I have spies, Beckett. The police, the judges, the media, not to mention the loyal cadre of patients who have gone through the Program. They're always looking out for me. Always." Peter punched his right hand skyward. "Rafferty, *aus! Fass! Fass!*"

Keek, keek, keek!

A shriek of pain echoed through the house and turned into a pathetic wail.

Keek, keek, keek!

Bodies wrestling. Shattering glass. Finally, a single gunshot.

Keek, keek, keek!

Silence.

Taylor covered her face with both hands, grinding her teeth in silent fear for her life.

With grace. With glory. With God's light.

Brooklyn scurried out of the church right after the end of Father McGavin's sermon. She sat cross-legged on the church's front lawn and opened the photo on her phone of the SUV in Taylor's driveway the night of her disappearance. She enlarged the image to make out the letters and numbers. But as it grew larger, the characters grew blurry, forcing her to lean in for focus.

"It's a pleasure to see you, Brooklyn."

Brooklyn pulled the phone away and glanced up to see Father McGavin smiling from above.

"How's your mother?" he asked.

"Oh, she's doing well, Father." Brooklyn stood and stuffed her phone into her pocket. "She's working a lot, has a case going to trial. But she's good. I'm sure she'll be here tomorrow. Thank you for asking, Father."

Father McGavin smiled. "May God bless you, Brooklyn."

"Thank you, Father." Brooklyn bowed her head. "Peace be with you."

"And also with you."

Brooklyn said goodbye and strode onto the sidewalk. When she turned the corner onto Prospect Street, she emailed the image of the car to herself. And then she ran home.

Once inside, she blew past her mom in the living room and straight into her bedroom, where she put to use that Photoshop elective she took last semester. Brooklyn converted the 350-kilobyte picture into a high-resolution file. Then opening up the new file, she enlarged the super-pixelated pic to make out the plate number: 2101ZZ.

She texted Holden.

can you run a license plate # for me?

no

????

it's illegal

????

in CA only licensed PI's or cops
have access. Sorry boo

blah. Ok. tx

Her mom appeared at the bedroom door. "Whatcha doin',
Sherlock Holmes?"

"Research," Brooklyn said casually.

"Researching sprinting? Because you ran in here like an
Olympian."

"Oh yeah." Brooklyn laughed. "I'm just a little obsessed with
a story, that's all."

"Can you share a little about it? I respect you need some
privacy, but I feel like I have no idea what you've been up to
lately. I love that you're loving the journalism and that you're
so good at it. It's a great hobby, Brookie. But, look, it's sad to
me that I have to check *Deadline Diaries* to find out what
you've been up to."

Brooklyn closed her laptop and got up and hugged her. "It's
okay, Mom. But you remember what the police told us when
they were still searching for Dad? They said they could only
share information on a 'need to know' basis because they
didn't want any facts to leak out that could possibly impede
their investigation. It's sort of the same with investigative journalism. I'm sure you understand."

"Maybe I can help. I'm pretty good at getting to the bottom of things."

"No, it's okay. Really."

"You sure?"

"Seriously, Mom. I appreciate it. But Holden has been really helpful. I'm good."

"I respect your need to maintain confidentiality about your stories. But as long as you are living in this house, I will not accept that when it comes to your personal life. So tell me about Tamara. Has she been helping you, too?"

"What do you mean?"

"You just answered my question with a question. Has Tamara been helping you? Yes or no?"

"Yes. She helped me."

"So that's why Mrs. Bailcy saw her pick you up on Wednesday night when I was at work?"

"Yes."

"And so tell me: Where did you go with my least favorite high school dropout?"

"To see a video."

"Where?"

"L.A."

Her mother's eyes bugged. "Los Angeles?"

"Yes."

Her mom parked her hands on her hips. "Wow." She shook her head with disgust. "This is the daughter I raised? Someone who hides things from me, who makes irresponsible choices like driving to L.A. with a girl you know I don't approve of? I don't know if I am more angry with you for violating my trust, or with myself for letting you become the kind of person who would do something so irresponsible."

Brooklyn's mom paced the bedroom. "Did Tamara take you partying or something while you were down there? I hear that's her M.O., that little troublemaker."

"No. She was actually doing me a favor. I'm the one who asked her to take me. I had a source who had a video to show me."

"And your source couldn't just email it to you?"

"No. It's complicated to explain, but—"

"Don't." Her mom put her hands in the "stop" position. "Don't talk."

Brooklyn nervously twisted her hair into pigtails. "You should be happy that I am working, doing something productive. You were the one who told me I need to get out of the house more."

"I would be supportive if I knew what the heck you were doing. But lately I have no idea what you are up to. You've become so closed off. I don't even know where you were today."

"Church! I was praying! So is that a crime, too?"

Her mom froze.

"I was praying to Dad for help. Because at least he always listened."

"I listen."

"But you don't hear me."

"What does that mean?"

"It means that you don't hear me when I tell you that I have no friends at school anymore and it makes me sad. You don't hear me when I tell you that Tamara isn't the bad person other people make her out to be. You don't listen when I tell you that Holden and Tamara are the only people in this world who truly understand me, who support me, who believe in what I am doing unconditionally."

"I don't think that's true, Brookie."

"See? There you go again! Look, everyone thinks I'm that sad little girl who lost her dad, who's lost in her sad little blog. They pity me. They think I am some sort of freak. But you are so obsessed with trying to convince me this isn't true that you aren't hearing the truth."

"You're an outlier, Brooklyn," her mom said. "It can be lonely when you're more advanced than everyone your age."

"Mom, I know. I've heard this speech a million times. Did it ever occur to you that maybe the reason why Tamara and Holden are the only two real friends I have is because they are also outcasts? Tamara's one of like five black kids in our school, and the only one who speaks her mind. Holden has been bullied since kindergarten. Call us outliers if you want. But it doesn't make it any easier on us."

"You're just advanced, Brooklyn."

"But how am I supposed to keep advancing if you just want to keep holding me back? You realize that in less than two years I'll be on my way to college? At some point you have to let me take risks. It's a lot of pressure on me to always be safe because I know that if anything ever happened to me you would just die and wouldn't be—"

Brooklyn paused, letting her tears curl around her chin and down her neck.

"I'm sorry." Brooklyn crashed backward onto her bed. "I'm a mess."

"I'm glad you're sorry." Her mother sniffled, wiping her own cheeks. "But I really think you need to take a break from that girl Tamara. She's just a bad influence."

"You're wrong about her. It was my idea—not hers. It's not her fault."

"You can work on your blog all you want. But you can't ride in a car with just anyone. That's too dangerous. You have to at least clear it with me first."

"Until when?"

"Until I say so."

Brooklyn shot up off the bed. "Is that you talking? Or the

bottles in the garbage?"

Her mom glared back at Brooklyn. "Nice try. You're deflecting. But we're talking about you, not me."

Brooklyn picked up a pillow and threw it across the room. She stomped past her mom. But as she stepped through the doorway, she stopped. Then she turned around, picked up the pillow, and arranged it perfectly back in its place on the bed. She marched out of the room and left her mom alone.

"Now squeeze." Nurse Mary Darling steadied the needle just above Taylor's tricep. "Just a little prick."

Taylor squeezed the rubber ball and grunted, the pain radiating up her arm as the fluid spread inside her veins. She glanced at the door and whispered, "I need you to contact my assistant, Simone. You need to tell her where I am."

Taylor handed the nurse a tiny scrap of paper with Simone's cell phone number scrawled on it. "Someone has been killed. Someone named Beckett. Peter shot him in Casa Bell. I heard it happen. Something needs to be done. Do the right thing. Please."

Nurse Mary stuffed the message into the pocket of her smock, pointed at the ceiling camera with her chin, and fussed with the medical cart in a normal fashion. "The guards change shifts every night at ten," she said in a hushed voice. She pressed a pack of bubblegum into the palm of Taylor's hand. "Jam this in the lock. When the guards change shifts, that's your chance. I cannot help any more."

The door to Taylor's room buzzed open. Taylor slid the gum under her pillow as the nurse jolted, quickly placing the used syringe onto her cart just as Peter bounded in wearing Birkenstocks.

"*Buenos dias*, Nurse Darling," Peter said. "*Cuál es el problema?*"

"*No hay problema.*"

"*Deje!*" he barked, telling her to leave. She bowed and quickly rolled the cart out of the room.

"Please excuse Nurse Darling's unprofessionalism," Peter told Taylor. "She knows better than to distract members with idle chitchat." He glanced down at his tablet. "I've been reading the staff reports on your progress. Your red blood cell count has improved markedly since your arrival last week. Your body mass index is already below a fifteen; you came here at eighteen percent. All together, we've seen a two-percent increase in muscle mass and four-percent decrease in fat. And we've gotten your hormone levels to much more optimal numbers. Your physical journey is on the right path." He took off his sunglasses. "But we've still got a problem."

"Is it my water intake? I'm sorry, but it makes me have to pee all the time—"

"No, no, no. We are pleased with your *physical* progress. It's a mental blockage. Based on the staff reports and my own observations, we fear you are resisting the Program. Now, it could be subconscious; I am not accusing you of anything. But, my dear, this is not good. Not for you, not for us. Not for the movement. Do you understand me?"

"I'm afraid, I don't."

"You simply need more Delete Sessions. As you have experienced with Helper Lily, they are typically verbal exercises. But when those aren't working, we must go to Level Two."

"Two?"

"Level one is verbal," he said. "Level two, electrical."

Taylor's stomach pinched tightly. "I promise I will do better, Dr. Kensington."

"For the last time, call me 'Peter,'" he said with a frown. "Dr. Kensington makes me feel old."

Peter sat in the chair beside Taylor's bed. "Let's give our verbal efforts another try, shall we? I will be performing this session myself. So just relax and close your eyes, Taylor. And as always, don't self-edit your replies. Simply respond with your first instinct."

"I'll do my best."

"Tell me about your father's death."

"I was eleven. He had skin cancer that spread."

"Please tell me, Taylor, what is rule number four of the Program?"

"I will avoid harmful sun exposure."

"Very good, Ms. Prince. You are indeed learning. So would it be a correct statement to say that the Program, if practiced, can save lives?"

"Yes, that would be accurate."

"So, your father, did he wear sunscreen?"

"Not really."

"But you still consider your father a mentor?"

"Yes."

"How so?"

"He was a hard worker. He was kind. He lived a life of love by example."

"Some example! An example of how to die too young? How to be self-destructive? An example of letting an easily preventable disease take his life?"

Taylor pinched her eyes tighter.

"Answer me, Taylor."

"He wasn't perfect, but he taught me a lot."

The whir from the air-conditioning vent hummed amid their silent standoff.

"Would you believe that studies show the greatest trauma a parent can inflict on a child is dying too young?" Peter asked.

"I would believe that to be true, yes."

"Would you believe the primary cause of most neuroses, most cases of high blood pressure, most stress-induced illnesses, is the deeply rooted trauma people have due to their fear of death?"

"Okay. If you say so."

"The data says so! You, Ms. Prince, must delete the memory you have of your father as a mentor—clinically, spiritually, intellectually, emotionally. The dark past that he painted is discoloring you. His deletion will open up a brighter future."

Taylor gnashed her molars.

"So when I say the words, 'Your father,' you will say, 'delete.'"

Taylor lay still, eyes closed.

"Your father," Peter said slowly.

Silence.

"Your father," he repeated, more loudly.

Silence.

"Your father!"

Taylor opened her eyes, lifted her head just up from the pillow, and flashed her million-dollar Hollywood smile. "Delete."

Uncle Don. Technically, retired detective Donald Gomez wasn't a blood uncle, but with the rest of her dad's relatives back in New York, Brooklyn's father's former partner had always served as an honorary one.

"Y'ello," Uncle Don answered his phone.

"Hey, it's Brooklyn!"

"Hey, kiddo. What's shakin', bacon?"

"I have a little favor to ask."

"Well, you've come to the right guy."

A year after his partner died, Uncle Don left the Twin Oaks force to start his own private investigation agency. Every month or so, Uncle Don would check in on Brooklyn; he had made that promise to her mother upon Kit's death.

"What can I do you for? How's the blog going? My daughter tells me you've become quite the reporter."

"Kind of. I'm trying."

"If you ain't tryin', you're dyin'," Don said. "And you know how much your dad hated to see you cry. He'd be very proud of you."

"Thank you. But, Uncle Don, I could use your help with something I'm working on."

He chuckled. "The last time I paid attention to celebrities, Burt Reynolds was a big movie star. But, you know, I am always here for you."

"So if I gave you a license plate number could you trace it to the owner of the vehicle?"

He laughed. "You're sounding like Kit more and more. Always hunting down someone, always kicking over rocks."

Though a lot of information was available to the public on the Web, a lot of information on individuals sat on databases only accessible to law enforcement and licensed private investigators. Mostly, Don tracked down witnesses for lawyers, ran background checks on executives, and conducted the occasional lie detector test. It was all pretty easy work for an FBI-trained investigator.

"The answer, my dear, is yes, of course I can. But it would just trace back to the registered owner, not necessarily the driver."

"That's okay. I'll take whatever I can get. I have been stuck on a story and I'm hoping this might break it open."

"What's the number?"

Brooklyn read him the number. "Can you keep this confidential?" she added.

"And by confidential, I assume you mean that I won't tell your mom."

Brooklyn crossed her fingers. "Um, yeah."

"I'll get that for you, no problem. But please do me a favor."

"Sure."

"Listen to your mom," he said. "She's a good lady. I know she's protective of you and that sometimes she can be wound tighter than a two-dollar watch, but she loves you very much. Understand me?"

"Yes."

"Alrighty then." Don sighed. "But you can't tell your mom I'm helping, either. If she found out, I'm sure the news would go over about as smoothly as a five-hundred-pound pole vaulter."

Taylor listened. She had grown so used to feigning interest during Peter's lectures that she had literally begun biting her tongue. As Taylor and Peter strolled side by side down a path that bisected the clinic's lush main lawn, the morning sun peeking over the mountains, he began: "I have a question for you. What do you think of me?"

"I think you are a very passionate person. And you're very intelligent. I am learning a lot from you. You've changed my life in so many ways," Taylor said.

A set of dimples broke through the tightly stretched skin of Peter's cheeks. "And what about my appearance? What do you make of it?"

"You are very fashionable." Taylor sized up his wrinkle-free white polo shirt and green slacks. "And fit."

"Thank you, my dear. You are very sweet."

"You asked."

He checked an app on his phone. "Four laps around this property total about ten thousand steps. And it looks as if we're just about halfway to our goal."

Taylor didn't deny that her diet and exercise program had done wonders for her physique. In fact, as she strode on the path she could feel butt muscles clenching that hadn't been there when she arrived some two weeks earlier. But despite the benefits of the Program, she remained freaked out by Peter's propaganda, crazy rants, and threats.

He draped his arm around her shoulders. "I have something else I'd like to discuss with you. We can be honest, you and I, can't we?"

She bowed her head. "No more secrets. No more lies. No

more traumas, only light."

"Good then. So I assume you heard the ruckus in the living room the other day."

Taylor hesitated, but offered a slow nod. The argument with Beckett, the talk of electroshock therapy and kidnapping, the screaming monkey, the gun shot. She'd hoped Peter had forgotten she was upstairs. He obviously hadn't.

"It's okay if you heard," Peter said. "It was a terrible incident. That boy attacked me, and I simply acted in self-defense."

"Yes, okay. If you say so, but I barely heard a thing. I thought someone dropped something."

"Nobody's perfect, Taylor," he said. "We all make mistakes. But we can learn from them. We have to confront our past and be ruthless in healing ourselves from what haunts us."

Peter gestured at a white wood bench. "Have a seat." When she did, he took a seat close beside her. And he leaned even closer. "I've never shared this with anyone else, but I feel as if you and I have a special connection. I think we understand each other because of our pasts."

"We all have a past," Taylor said "It makes us human. It's okay."

"My mother died when I was thirteen. And my father was a scientist, always either obsessed with his lab or obsessed with the drink. Children need their parents' attention, they need to feel as though someone is caring for them. To me, there is nothing more precious than a child. In their innocence, children express so much light and love."

"That's a beautiful perspective," Taylor said. "I agree. So true."

"But sadly, that beauty gets corrupted."

"How so?"

"By adults, by time, by society in general. We live in a sick, sick world. We live in a world where children are abandoned, abused, exploited. We live in a world where youthfulness is valued, but the aged are discarded like a disease. And it *is* a disease, though not one for which a person should be punished. This is the disease of our time. Fortunately, I believe I have found the cure."

Peter got up and began pacing, kicking the pebbles on the path. "Fifteen is a magic number, Taylor. It's when one becomes psychologically, emotionally, and biologically equipped to survive. But it's also what I call 'The Negative Pivot Age.' After fifteen, the incidence of an assortment of diseases increases dramatically. And my studies show it's also when one's appearance becomes less youthful, less objectively attractive."

Taylor swallowed hard.

Peter continued, "The skin starts to sag, stretch marks appear, and metabolism slows, making it harder to maintain the kind of idealized physical beauty we've come to fetishize. That's when society begins to judge, to discard its aged in Darwinian fashion. Fifteen, Taylor. To be forever fifteen is to feel forever vital and alive. We have the science to achieve this. We now know how to achieve this state of perfection."

Taylor sat, hands folded in her lap. She noticed that Peter was talking at her, not *to* her. His agitated gaze pierced through her and into an almost imaginary person—perhaps the ghosts of the past that haunted him. Like a madman. Intelligent, yes. Articulate, definitely. Passionate, to be sure. But a madman, nonetheless.

"I couldn't be more dedicated to this cause." Peter's voice cracked with emotion, as if he could break down in tears. "All I'm doing—I should say 'we' because you are part of this revolution of human potential—is piecing it together in one simple easy-to-follow program. Potentially, we can revolutionize the very way human beings experience life. We no longer will have mid-life crises to battle. We no longer will spend hundreds of billions on health care to treat the sick and dying. That money could be spent on enhancing and lengthening our lives. An ounce of prevention is worth a pound of cure. This is not a new idea. But it is an idea that's time has come."

Sweat formed on his upper lip and forehead. He took off his straw hat, combed back his now moist hair, and exhaled. Then he put his hat back on. "People have created religions, fabricated a false God and gods, and concocted these biblical myths. They profess these stories as fact, simply so they can cope with the fundamental fear that their lives are short. Physical immortality would make these fear-based dogmas obsolete."

Peter placed his hand on Taylor's thigh, and she rolled her leg inward. She stopped short of slapping his hand. "You can trust me, my child," he assured her with a smile. "Have you read the Bible, Taylor?"

She wasn't sure which was the "right" answer.

"It's nothing to be ashamed of. I am sure it was forced on you, just like it was on the rest of us when we were children." Peter licked his lips. "Do you remember the first commandment?"

"Thou shalt not kill?" guessed Taylor, who had been dragged to church by her grandparents just a handful of times.

Peter laughed. "No, my child. That would certainly make more sense—to place, first and foremost above everything else, the preservation of life as the most important rule to follow? But that's not the hypocrites' very first commandment. Instead it is, 'You shall have no other gods but me.'"

Peter sprang to his feet. "Oh, how convenient for God that his first command is about the almighty Him! Talk about narcissism! Talk about paternalistic order! The Peter Kensington Program will not only expose religion for being ancient fiction, it will also spark the New Enlightenment."

He stopped pacing and crouched down toward Taylor, his face close enough she could smell his aftershave. "The mind, Taylor. I believe that when the Program is adopted *en masse* it will usher in an era of modern *thought*. From that will spring a belief system in which we, the People, are God. Without the shackles of historical religion, we will have no more holy wars, no more religious oppression, no more dogma-fueled gender and sexual discrimination. Logic and science will have won. Scientific research no longer will suffer from these shackles of repressive, anti-intellectual religious institutions. Indeed, Taylor, the Program teaches us that the power of God can be found within all of us."

She noticed the way the doctor's pupils got tiny when he got into his preaching mode, seemingly without taking a breath. She could only conclude that Dr. Peter Kensington, although fit and youthful looking for a man soon to be pushing fifty, could not be of sound mind.

Peter dropped down on the bench. "This music video project you and Evan will be shooting this coming week is very important." He wiped his forehead with his handkerchief. "I need you to do this for me. I need you to commit a hundred percent to our mission. Together, Taylor, we can change the world."

Brooklyn yawned. And with that she began her daily routine of checking the Hollywood blogs and Twitter on her laptop, where she was greeted by a photo featuring a wide-smiling girl with a buzz cut in a hospital bed flashing two enthusiastic thumbs pointing skyward.

The photo from *STARSTALK* was accompanied by the tweet, *Update: Taylor Prince Still on Mend in Rehab*. No link to a story. No more information. Just a photo. *Smart move*. Whoever was holding Taylor, if indeed they were still keeping her, would invite more questions if they released too much information. But a single image depicting her happy and recovering, her shaven head remaining, could represent a powerful piece of propaganda.

Brooklyn realized that the vast majority of the 7,567,984 followers of *STARSTALK*'s Twitter account, including other media members, likely viewed the pic as evidence of yet another pathetic celebrity train wreck who had gone away to a high-priced rehab. Celebrity PR 101 suggested that leaked photos showing the celebrity in a positive light served as a necessary step in the rehabilitation of their image. It was a fundamental step in what had become the Hollywood comeback cliché.

But no one who saw the pic that morning knew what Brooklyn did. They hadn't seen the security footage of Taylor being carried away in that SUV. They hadn't heard the confessions of Pretty Boy Beckett. And they hadn't interviewed her assistant, Simone Witten, and heard her eyewitness account of Taylor's sudden disappearance.

Brooklyn scanned the photo. She could see Taylor's left mid-arm was connected to a clear IV tube, which snaked up to a drip bag, on which was printed in fancy green lettering, "Kensington."

When *STARSTALK* had broken the story of Taylor allegedly being sent to rehab, it had only identified her as being at an "undisclosed addiction treatment center" in California.

Brooklyn scoured the search engines with keyword combinations. Kensington + IV bags + medical equipment + rehabs . . . Nothing. She even checked online to see if Kensington was among the state's registered addiction treatment centers. Again, nothing.

Bling! An incoming email alert. She clicked open the new message:

From: Mallory Barrie, Event Publicist

To: Brooklyn Brant

Subject: Media Invite For Red Carpet Event

You have been selected to be among the exclusive list of media invited to cover the red carpet arrivals of the fifth annual Hero Awards Gala tonight at 6 p.m. at the Beverly Hilton. The annual gala, organized by the non-profit Kensington Solutions, recognizes true heroes in the world of media, entertainment, politics, and law enforcement who have made a valuable contribution to promoting values and images that positively impact children and young adults. Celebrity and VIP red carpet arrivals begin at 5:30 p.m. You've also been approved for a one-on-one interview with celebrity attendee Evan Ryan. Please RSVP to reserve your spot on the carpet for this exclusive black-tie event by replying to this email.

VIP AND CELEBRITY ATTENDEES AVAILABLE FOR INTERVIEWS INCLUDE:

EVAN RYAN, Actor
L.A. Police Superintendent HARRY WARD
JONATHAN LIVINGSTON, Supervisor of California State Prisons and Rehabilitation
L.A. Superior Court JUDGE RONALD OPIN
BLAKE EDWARD, Starlight Movie Studios CEO
L.A. Mayor LUIS SUAREZ
EMILY LAMONT, *STARSTALK* Executive Editor

Brooklyn often received invitations to cover red carpets, which she almost always declined. Reporters rarely broke news through fluffy, publicist-managed red carpet interviews. But this event could be different. Not because of the presence of cops and politicians and wealthy donors, but due to the presence of one celebrity, Evan Ryan.

Earlier in the year, the actor had been rumored to be dating Taylor Prince. He had also reportedly gone to rehab. Other sources close to Taylor so far hadn't delivered a newsbreak. Beckett had gone off the grid for almost a week. Taylor's manager, publicist, and agent—all of whom had fed Brooklyn anonymous tips and information over the years—no longer returned her emails and calls. Simone had passed along Evan Ryan's email and cell that first day she and Brooklyn had met. But Evan had never returned her repeated, pestering reach-outs.

To: Mallory Barrie

From: Brooklyn Brant

Re: Media Invite For Red Carpet Event

Thank you for the invitation. I would love to cover the event, and would like to schedule a one-on-one interview with Evan Ryan. Please let me know if we are confirmed for tonight.

Then Brooklyn texted Holden.

covering my FIRST red carpet event tonight. Might get Evan Ryan. Need an 'assistant.' ☺ Wanna join?

Brooklyn felt a strong urge to commence the Fourmation. But this moment, this vital point in her pursuit of what could be the biggest story of her journalism career, required even more drastic measures.

She grabbed her Bible from the nightstand, where passages she had interpreted with the mention of fours were lined over with a pink highlighter. Then she closed her eyes as if spinning a roulette wheel, and opened to a random page.

No pink section.

She closed the Bible, and again her eyes, before opening it again. This time she landed on one of her Fourmation favorites, Psalm 107. Brooklyn had identified the chapter as the only one in the Bible that contained the exact same phrase four times.

She read aloud the line each of the times it appeared in verse:

Verse 8: "Let them praise the LORD for his great love and for the wonderful things he has done for them."

Verse 15: "Let them praise the LORD for his great love and for the wonderful things he has done for them."

Verse 21: "Let them praise the LORD for his great love and for the wonderful things he has done for them."

Verse 31: "Let them praise the LORD for his great love and for the wonderful things he has done for them."

Brooklyn didn't care what others might have called her ritual. She only cared that during her seventeenth recitation of the line, her laptop alerted her to a new email message—the publicist confirming a one-on-one with Evan Ryan at 5 p.m. later that day. And she felt a sense of purpose and direction and grace that Father McGavin might call "the Holy Spirit."

"Trust me." Peter guided Taylor back to Casa Bell. "This project is much, much more than just a music video."

"I know, I've read the treatment," Taylor said. "It's very dramatic. Dreamy."

"So then you get it."

"I think so. Like you said, it's basically a retelling of *Peter Pan* set to the 'Forever Young' song. Two young lovers. A girl—me—who is turning sixteen and doesn't want to grow up, meets a boy who promises to make her wish come true."

"Yes, that is the general narrative. But what I'm wondering is whether you get the *bigger picture*? Whether you understand why you've gotten the role of Wendy."

"I understand it's promoting the values of the Program, if that's what you're getting at."

"Not entirely. What I'm getting at is that you are the Chosen One."

"The Chosen One?"

Peter took Taylor's right hand in his.

"Why me?"

"Because you're young. Because you're famous. Because you're intelligent. Because you're of sturdy body and mind, yet also elegant and beautiful. That makes you perfect for the role. I didn't choose you."

"I don't understand."

"I didn't choose you, Taylor." He pointed past the Kensington walls. "They chose you! The public's fascination with you. And now fate has brought us together. Your troubles landed you here in my lap, but your rehabilitation through the Program will inspire the world. Because, just like Jesus, celebrities are symbols. You can use that responsibility to sell movie tickets, to market a fragrance, or to sell shampoo. But that's not very godly, that's not befitting the Chosen One."

The pair got to the front gate of the main house. Peter buzzed open the door and led Taylor to the front porch swing. "There's something so liberating about a swing, so childlike. In a small way, it's like experiencing the sensation of flight."

"Like Peter Pan?" Taylor asked as she swayed.

"Yes, just like him, the man who lived as a boy. And when he taught Wendy how to fly, she felt that freedom. In a way, I suppose, all I am really doing is teaching you how to fly."

"When will I be able to fly on my own?"

"Soon. But only when you've earned your wings. Tuesday is a big day. For you and Evan."

"Where is Evan? I was hoping to rehearse a little with him before the shoot."

"He's making a public appearance in service of the Program. He's on a mission to tie up some loose ends. Tonight he will earn *his* wings."

"You look . . ." Holden's eyes bugged as he struggled to find the right word. "Like, um, a—"

"A girl?" Brooklyn finished his sentence with a grin.

Made up with heavy eye shadow, lipstick, and a tight-fitting black cocktail dress, she stood in front of Holden in her living room. Her silver cross necklace rested flat on the center of her chest while expertly curled hair cascaded down each shoulder.

"Soooo?" Brooklyn urged playfully. "What were you gonna say I looked like? And please don't say a hooker because I borrowed this dress from my mother."

"You look like a celebrity," Holden said. "You look famous or something."

Brooklyn blushed. "Aw, thanks, Holdy. And you look very handsome in that tux." She like-so adjusted his bow tie. "We're going to make quite the red carpet duo."

"The *Deadline Diaries* duo," he said.

"Okay, kids," Brooklyn's mom said over-enthusiastically as she stepped into the room. She had apparently rushed home from work to take in the moment her tomboy daughter decided to play dress-up.

Brooklyn rolled her eyes. "It's a red carpet, Mom—not a prom."

"But you guys look far too adorable not to document." Her mother framed them with her phone. "Okay. Look here. What's a mouse eat?"

Brooklyn slung her arm around Holden and flashed a "*cheeeeeese*" smile.

"Drive safely," her mother instructed Holden before wrapping Brooklyn in a tight hug. "And good luck, Brookie. I'll say a prayer for you."

Brooklyn pecked her mom on the cheek. "Thanks. I'll do my best."

Her mom waved goodbye from the front step as Brooklyn hopped into the passenger seat of Holden's car. Unlike Tamara and her beater Toyota, Holden and his father's BMW four-door sedan were much more trustworthy in her mother's eyes.

During the nearly two-hour drive down to Los Angeles, Brooklyn obsessively went over her questions for Evan Ryan, tapping them into her cell's notepad as she practiced them on Holden. Her strategy: Butter up Evan by asking him about the gala and why he was attending. Then she'd ask about his next movie project. She didn't want to begin with any touchy questions—like, say, about the whereabouts and condition of Taylor Prince. She had learned from her father the art of interrogation: avoid questions that could be answered with a simple "yes" or "no." She planned on ending the interview with a simple question: "How is Taylor doing?"

"Sounds good," Holden said, keeping his eyes on the freeway ahead. "That way, if he gets mad, or the publicist stops the interview, at least we got something from him on tape."

"Just remember that no matter what happens, don't stop recording."

Holden pulled into the palm-lined driveway of the Beverly Hilton a little after four thirty, a half hour before her interview with Evan. Brooklyn had only seen the legendary hotel when watching the Golden Globes on TV.

A uniformed valet attendant opened the passenger door for Brooklyn. Careful not to create a wardrobe malfunction for the paparazzi lurking on the sidewalk, she gingerly stepped out of the car. A woman in a white blouse and black pantsuit wearing a headset approached her.

"Brooklyn Brant?" The woman checked her clipboard. "*Deadline Diaries*?"

Brooklyn pushed her scrunched-up dress down into place and extended her hand. "That's me!"

"Mallory Barrie," the woman said, shaking hands. "Happy to have you cover our event tonight. You might be the youngest reporter I've ever had on a red carpet. How old are you?"

"Sixteen," she said, "and a half."

Brooklyn looked over at Holden, who had a camera bag slung over his shoulder and was pulling a tripod from the trunk of his car.

"Is that your shooter?" Mallory asked.

"Yes, that's Holden."

"My assistant will set him up at your position on the rope line," Mallory said. "You're in the first online slot, just behind *E! News* and *Access Hollywood*. While he's setting up on the red carpet, I'll take you up to the room for your sit-down."

Brooklyn tilted her head. "But, uh, I need Holden to shoot my interview."

"Sorry," Mallory said. "I've been ordered that cameras are restricted to the carpet only. I apologize that this wasn't made more clear. Your interview will be for print only."

Brooklyn pursed her lips. "Fine." She turned to Holden. "Meet you later on the carpet, Holden."

"Come with me, Ms. Brant." Brooklyn followed the publicist into the hotel, across the marble floor of the bustling lobby to the bank of elevators.

"We've been keeping it under wraps, but Evan is being honored tonight," Mallory explained as they waited for the next lift. "He's receiving the Young Leader award. As you know, he's had his run-ins with the law and credits the legal system for helping to get him scared straight. He will be giving a very moving speech. It's going to be a special night."

Brooklyn followed her into the empty elevator. Mallory barked into her headset, "We're coming up."

"I have to ask," Brooklyn said as the door closed, "did Evan personally approve my interview with him? Does he know that *Deadline Diaries* is interviewing him? This isn't something I would normally do."

Mallory beamed. "Sweetie, not only did he approve, but he personally requested that you interview him. In fact, you're his only one-on-one. He isn't even walking the red carpet. This is his only media interview tonight."

"And his first since rehab."

"Oh yes. About that . . ." The doors spread open to the seventh floor. They both stepped out. "No personal questions. We'd like to keep the interview focused on the event."

"My job as a journalist is to ask. His job as the subject is to decide whether or not to answer." Brooklyn had never agreed to any restrictions before and wasn't about to agree to any now. "That's only fair."

"Ms. Brant," Mallory said. "I'm just a volunteer for this nonprofit and I am telling you what the organizers told me. Just, please, keep it professional."

A credible journalist never agrees to ground rules.

Mallory led Brooklyn to the very end of the hall to a set of double doors guarded by a hulking man in a dark suit and sunglasses. The guard's arms were nearly as wide as Brooklyn's torso, which he scanned head to toe, leering at her low-cut dress to the point where she felt uncomfortable.

Brooklyn cleared her throat. "Can I help you?" The guard looked familiar to her, like one of those WWE wrestlers. But everyone in L.A. looked like someone. "Brooklyn Brant."

"She's cleared," Mallory assured the guard.

The guard nodded and inserted a card key into the entry slot. He swiped it back out and pushed the door open. "He's ready for you. You've got five minutes."

As Brooklyn crossed through the entry, the guard stuck out

his arm, blocking Mallory from following her inside. "One on one," he grumbled. "Not two on one."

The heavy hotel door closed behind her and Brooklyn stood alone in the suite. The shades were drawn, but floor lamps and a crystal chandelier brightened the room. The suite bent into an L shape to the right.

Brooklyn peeked her head around the corner. "Hello?"

"Coming!" a male voice sounded from the bedroom.

Four vases. Four chairs in the corner of the suite. Four side tables. 5:04 p.m. Brooklyn stopped herself. She didn't want the Fourmation to distract her from what was the most important interview of her career. She wanted to prove to herself that she could be normal, a professional.

Focus. She sucked in a deep breath and recited a silent prayer.

Evan appeared from the bedroom in a perfectly tailored tux—shorter than he looked in pictures and thinner than she'd ever seen him. She noticed dark circles under his eyes and his skin had the pastiness of someone who had not seen much sun.

"*The* Brooklyn Brant?" he joked with a smile.

"*The* Evan Ryan?" she joked back.

"How about we do this on the balcony? It's private." He spoke in a blunt monotone, as if he had just woken up from a nap. "Please, let's step outside."

He opened the sliding glass door and stepped onto the balcony overlooking downtown Beverly Hills. She sat in the chair beside him.

"*Deadline Diaries* is a very good website," Evan said. "You've got a good reputation in Hollywood. You should know that. And thanks for always being fair to me."

"I try to be fair to everyone," Brooklyn replied. "Or at least I try my best."

Evan stared off into the hazy distance. "I have one ground rule—"

"Don't worry. I'm aware I shouldn't ask any personal questions, but like I told Mallory, I have to ask what I have to ask. You can answer as you wish. I just can't ethically agree to do an interview under that kind of restriction."

"We're not doing an interview," he sighed. "That's definitely not happening."

"Then why am I even here?"

Evan reached back for the glass door and closed it.

"We are talking." His voice, his expression, his posture turned stiff. "Privately." He leaned forward, resting his elbows on his thighs. "This all has to be off the record."

Her creep-o-meter on alert, Brooklyn slid her finger over her phone screen, unlocking it. Just in case she needed to make a call for help.

"How's Taylor doing?" she said, instantly abandoning her strategy of buttering him up.

Evan leaned back in the chair and crossed his arms. "Good question. But your question assumes I really know how she is doing."

"That's because I think you do. You guys were pretty close there for a while. Logic would tell me you have to know something."

He laughed. "Oh, really. Okay, let me ask you a question. Have you ever lied?"

"Of course."

"And it probably makes you feel bad?"

"Let's just say there's no guilt like Catholic guilt. Sunday school every week from the time I was in kindergarten. And Catholic school until my freshman year. So, yes, lying is a sin and I don't ever feel good about it."

"I'm jealous," Evan said.

"Of my guilt?"

"No, of your faith."

"I didn't always believe. It's kind of grown with me as I've gotten older."

"I don't know what I believe in anymore." His hands fidgeted. "I mean, all the pain and suffering in the world. All the evil people. All the death. Where is God in all that?"

"He's in all of it," she said. "The good and the bad."

"No offense, but I don't want to believe in a God that lets so much evil happen."

"Well, God said, 'I will punish the world for its evil, the wicked for their sins.'"

"Where did he say that?" Evan asked.

"Isaiah, chapter thirteen," she said. "Verse eleven."

"Wow!" He laughed. "Are you like a minister or something?"

"No, just Sunday school every week since kindergarten. And Catholic school, until my freshman year."

"Maybe that's my problem. While you were reading the Bible, I was reading scripts. While you were praying, I was memorizing lines. Now look at me. I'm lost. I've turned into the kind of person I would never have wanted to be by the time I was this age. I'm tired."

Brooklyn cocked her head. "What are you tired of?"

Evan focused his bloodshot eyes on her. "Tired of keeping secrets, of lying. Tired of people getting hurt." He stood and leaned his chest against the balcony's metal railing. "The truth is the only solution."

Brooklyn gripped her phone.

"This is not a game," he continued. "This is not about make-believe, not about Hollywood gossip. This is real—life and death."

"I don't understand."

"I was sent here to lie. I was sent here to lie in my speech to all those cops, all the media. I was sent here to lie to you,

Brooklyn. I'm supposed to tell you that Taylor is doing just great, that she's getting better and closer to making a comeback so that you will write a story about it and spread their lies." He looked down at the sidewalk. "And I've been told that if I don't lie to you, there will be consequences."

She swallowed. "You can tell me the truth. I will protect you. It's okay."

Evan stepped away from the railing. "Before I came here today, they reminded me that Whitney Houston died in this hotel. The story is that she was an addict and drowned in the bathtub in Room 434. They found pills in her room. The police called it 'an accident.'"

He leaned in closer to her ear and whispered, "They also said Michael Jackson's death was an accident. But nothing with these people is ever an accident."

Brooklyn sat rigid, at full attention.

"You know that guard out there?" Evan said. "He has a gun. I don't know what he will do with it, what so-called accident could happen. And I can't promise you what will happen to Taylor if I say the wrong thing. Time is running out. Any day now, after they're done using her, they will hurt her, just like they did me. Do you understand?"

"Are you saying you know who has Taylor? You know what rehab she's in?" Brooklyn asked.

He nodded yes.

"Is it Kensington?"

His eyes darted back through the glass door and he nodded. "How did you know?"

"I know quite a bit," she bluffed. "Is she okay?"

He slowly shook his head and looked down. "They call it 'Deletion.' If you resist, they fry your brain, so you'll submit. And so you'll forget."

"Forget what?"

"Your past self."

Brooklyn leaned in closer. "If all this is true, why aren't you telling the cops? There's probably a hundred police downstairs in that ballroom right now. Certainly, they could save her—and arrest the people responsible."

"Because the cops are in on it, Brooklyn. They're all bought off. That's how he's able to recruit so many celebrities. Cops, judges, DAs, publicists, tabloids, prison guards. Anyone who will take his money—bribes, blackmail." He released a pocket of air. "Brooklyn, it's bigger than just me, and bigger than Taylor. He's been running this cult—and it is definitely a *cult*—in Hollywood for a very long time. He calls it the Program. He claims he's helping people, ridding them of addictions and infusing them with health and wellness and, in his ultimate dream, immortal youth."

Brooklyn shook her head. "You realize how crazy this all sounds, don't you? I'm not saying you're lying, but honestly, what you're telling me is highly illegal, unethical, and plain evil. I need verifiable proof that a) Taylor is there and b) She is undergoing treatment against her will. I need you to go on the record."

"I can't go on the record," he said. "He will destroy me."

"Sounds like he's already doing that."

Evan and Brooklyn flinched at the thud of the inside suite door slamming shut. Evan quickly reached into his pocket and stuffed a folded scrap of paper into her hand, shielding them with his tuxedo-clad body. Brooklyn wedged open the top of her dress and placed the paper firmly in her cleavage. The bodyguard yanked open the glass door and barked, "Interview's over. Let's go." The guard glanced at Evan. "You all done here?"

Lifting his chin to the guard, Evan flashed Brooklyn a knowing wink. "She knows the real story. Right, Brooklyn?" He smiled.

"Yes," she affirmed. "Thanks for setting the record straight."

The bodyguard led Brooklyn out of the room and down the hall back to the elevators. "Enjoy your evening," he said.

"Oh, I will. It's been a real revelation."

The elevator bell pinged and the "down" light illuminated. "Bye!" Brooklyn waved as the doors closed. She immediately dug out the piece of paper and read the scrawled message: "Coachella Valley Vista Point—This Friday @ sunset."

As the doors opened, Brooklyn folded the paper back up and texted Holden.

Let's go. Now!

What? Whyyyyy?

Breaking news!!!! I'll explain ltr, lets go.

She sunk into a soft chair in the lobby and checked her email. The newest one had come within the hour from Uncle Don.

From: Donald Gomez

To: Brooklyn Brant

Date: August 14 at 5:33:58 PM PDT

Subject: URGENT CALL ME

Dear Brooklyn,

Ran the plate. Registered owner of vehicle is Kensington Solutions, a non-profit organization founded by a Peter Kensington. I ran a few searches for you. Some interesting and, frankly, disturbing results. I think we should chat after you read the report. CALL me, sweetie.—Uncle Don

"My child." Peter stuck his head into the upstairs bedroom where Taylor lay reading the "Forever Young" treatment in preparation for their video shoot. "Evan's speech is on the live stream."

Growing up, Wednesday evenings were when Taylor, her sister, and her parents would cuddle on the couch to watch reruns of *America's Funniest Home Videos*. Her dad said it was the best cure for the "hump day blues." As she followed Peter downstairs, all Taylor could think of was how she would have done anything to be back in Arizona laughing with her family at something as mundane as corny videos clips.

Peter led Taylor to the parlor, where he settled into a black leather chair. He gestured for Taylor to take a seat on the sofa beside him.

"Big night," he said. "His coming out!"

Taylor bit down on her lower lip, a nervous habit that directors always tried—and failed—to make her break. Good thing, as it became her trademark expression. Fans had dedicated memes to her infamous lip-biting pose.

Fans.

What had her fans thought of her dropping off the face of the Earth?

"Do my fans know where I am?" she asked.

"A statement was released saying you are receiving treatment and soon will be back and better than ever."

"Can I see the statement?"

"Yes, you can," he said. "In due time. Now it is time to focus on the Work."

"Do you have any children?"

"No, I don't. I don't want to bring children into this world, at least not until it is a healthier place to live, until we rid the world of its toxic lifestyles and damaging dogmas." Peter turned up a smile. "Until then, you and Evan—and the rest who you will inspire to join our movement—will be my children."

Peter picked up the remote control and clicked on the giant TV screen. It lit up with a live shot of the Beverly Hilton ballroom. A minute later, a woman in a black satin ball gown took the stage: Emily Lamont, *STARSTALK*'s Executive Editor.

"As a journalist covering Hollywood, we must often report on the unfortunate, yet inevitable, foibles of the rich and famous. The young man I am about to introduce to you is no stranger to *STARSTALK*. He is a young man who was arrested earlier this year for a DUI and was found to be in possession of illegal drugs. But his story has a happy ending. Rather than becoming yet another celebrity stuck in the revolving rehab door, this young man got real help. And it may never have happened if it weren't for the intervention of our friends in the Los Angeles police community. This young man has not only turned himself around, but he has also decided to publicly thank the men and women in this room who helped scare him straight. Ladies and gentlemen, receiving tonight's Hollywood Leadership Award, actor Mr. Evan Ryan."

Evan took the stage to a round of applause, accepting a plaque from Lamont. "I'm here tonight to share something very important," he read from a prompter. "I want to share a secret. It is something that I have never said in public. It is that I am an addict. I have demons that, if not treated, control me. But unlike the person I was just a few months ago, I am now freed from those demons. They no longer torture me. That's because I got help. And part of my recovery—a very big part— is a result of the law enforcement community.

"Had I never been arrested, had I never been ordered by a court to get help, I might even be dead. But tonight I stand before you more alive than ever. Over the coming months, I will be sharing more about my journey back from the brink, and revealing more about the Program that is responsible for it.

"But tonight is not for that. Rather, tonight is about you—the people in the media, in the courts, and in the world of law and justice. So it is with a grateful heart that I accept your award. It is because of you that I can stand before you a rejuvenated person with a light that will shine forever."

Peter wiped his eyes with his handkerchief. "Inspiring. Isn't it?"

Smile and nod.

"Oh, wow!" Brooklyn stared at her phone, mouth agape. "Unbelievable."

"What?" Minutes away from the Beverly Hilton, Holden steered his BMW down the carpool lane back to Twin Oaks. "Tell me!"

"Uncle Don." She finger-scrolled down through the report. "He traced that SUV's license plate. He found the owner. Wow."

FOR INFORMATIONAL PURPOSES ONLY

Report processed by:
GOMEZ INVESTIGATIONS INC.

FULL NAME	ADDRESS	COUNTY	PHONE
Kensington, Peter	789 62nd Ave	San Bernardino	Not listed
(AKA "Oliver Franks"	Thermal, CA 92274		
possible alias)			

ADDITIONAL PERSONAL INFORMATION

SSN	DOB	GENDER
097-45-XXXX	6/1970	M

CRIMINAL/CIVIL FILINGS—2 RECORDS FOUND

1: CALIFORNIA CRIMINAL COURT REPORT

OFFENDER INFORMATION
Name: KENSINGTON, PETER
(AKA OLIVER FRANKS)
Address: CA
Case Number: B24383
Case Filing Date: 08/02/1999
County: LA
DOB: 06/1970
SSN: 097-45-XXXX

OFFENSES
Case Filing Date: 08/02/1999
Offense Date: 07/28/1999
Court Case Number: B24383
Court Offense: Penal Code 288 (Felony)
Court Disposition Date: 10/26/1999

COURT ACTIVITY
[10/26/1999—Case dismissed]

* * *

2: CALIFORNIA CIVIL COURT REPORT

OFFENDER INFORMATION
Name: KENSINGTON, PETER
(AKA OLIVER FRANKS)
Address: CA
Case Number: 567890
Case Filing Date: 03/03/2002
County: SAN_BERNARDINO
DOB: 06/1970
SSN: 097-45-XXXX

OFFENSES
Case Filing Date: 03/03/2001
: Cal. Civ. Code § 1714(a)
Court Statute:

COURT ACTIVITY
[10/26/2002—Case dismissed]

"The car is registered to a non-profit called Kensington Solutions, based out in the desert," Brooklyn said. "That charity is run by a Peter Kensington, who has an alias of Oliver Franks. Weird. Beckett and Evan . . . it's all totally making sense now. They must have been talking about this Peter Kensington guy."

"What did Evan tell you exactly?"

Brooklyn relayed their hushed conversation on the hotel balcony.

"He looked like he hadn't slept in days and he just seemed to be so out of it."

"Like on drugs?" Holden asked.

"Not really. More like woozy, dazed. Maybe a little brain-damaged or something. He didn't seem right in the head." She smacked the dashboard with her fist. "That's it! Evan started talking about how these people could 'fry' Taylor's brain or something. Maybe that's what happened to him."

"Why didn't you ask him for details?"

"I was about to, but then the bodyguard came storming in. That's when Evan handed me this." Brooklyn held up the crumpled scrap of Beverly Hilton stationery and read aloud, "Coachella Valley Vista Point—Friday night @ sunset."

"Coachella?" Holden asked. "Like, the music festival?"

"Holdie, my dear. He's cute, but I highly doubt he was inviting me to Coachella. Plus, that's in the spring."

"Either way, I think we should call the cops now."

"Hell no!" Brooklyn looked up "Coachella Valley Vista" on her phone as she spoke. "I don't know enough about this rehab place, this Kensington guy, and what he may or may not be doing with Taylor. It's all hearsay. For all I know, it could be a legitimate rehab, or it could be something more deranged like Evan and Beckett have said. On top of that, Evan claims the police are in on it, like it's some huge conspiracy."

"Even more reason to alert the police," Holden insisted. "We can call Chief Price right now. I highly doubt this Peter Kensington guy has any influence over the Twin Oaks police force. They will help us."

"Don't get me wrong. I love Chief Price, but after we tell him, then what would he do? He'd just call down to L.A. because it's not his jurisdiction. It's too risky. Plus, I need to break this story first."

"You're way overthinking this case, Brooklyn."

"When it comes to investigative journalism," she said without looking up from her phone, "there's no such thing as overthinking. And by the way, Holden, it is a *story*—not a case. Detectives handle cases; journalists pursue stories."

"You think Taylor could be at this Coachella spot?"

"That would make the most sense." Brooklyn punched in a number and pressed her phone to her ear.

"Uncle Don!" she said.

"Hey, Brookie. I take it you got my email."

"Yes. Thank you." She flicked on speakerphone.

"Look, sweetie." Uncle Don's voice turned more serious. "I don't know what purpose you had in having me trace that vehicle, or what you want to know about this Peter Kensington guy. But I've spent my life dealing with criminals, and I just want to make sure you're aware of some things before you do anything more. Mainly, this fellow Kensington's history. See that offense from 1999?"

She scanned the report until she found it. "Yeah. What's Penal Code 288?"

"That's the thing. P.C. 288 is a felony. It means he was charged with committing lewd acts on a minor under age fourteen."

"'Lewd'?"

"Child molestation. Reading between the lines, looks like this Kensington guy might be a pedophile."

Brooklyn and Holden locked eyes across the front seat.

"Keep in mind," Uncle Don continued, "the report says his case was dismissed, which means there's a chance they could have been false charges, or maybe the D.A. found a lack of evidence to prosecute the case. Sadly, this happens a lot. These kinds of allegations can be too hard to prove guilt beyond a reasonable doubt, especially if it comes down to a kid's word versus the adult. But again, with this Kensington guy, it's hard to say either way. And since it involves a minor, those court records are sealed. We have no way of gaining access to the evidence or knowing who the victim was."

"What about the civil court case?" Brooklyn asked.

"He was sued for negligence. But the case was dismissed. Usually this means the parties settled it privately. The details would be in the lawsuit."

"That's public record, right?"

"Sure is," he said. "But to see it, you have to actually go the courthouse and pull the case file, which my firm can do for you. But honestly, if I am going to do any more work on this I would have to tell your mom. Tracing the owner of a car is one thing, but investigating an accused pedophile doctor, now that's—"

"Oh no, don't worry," Brooklyn said. "I don't need you to do anything more. You have helped enough. I was just curious."

"You sure?"

"Positive. Hundred percent."

"I'm always here if you need me."

"I know you are."

"Just do me a favor, Brookie."

"Okay."

"Just be careful."

When she hung up, Holden exploded, "Why didn't you have him help you?"

"Because my mom will just freak out and get in the way."

"Your mom's a lawyer, Brooklyn. She could get that lawsuit for you."

"That lawsuit is more just background—far from the most important thing here. And I can do this on my own anyway. I want to show my mom that *Deadline Diaries* is more than just a gossip site."

"That's fine," Holden said. "But I still think the police are better at this kind of thing."

"Oh, really?" Brooklyn glared at Holden. "If the police were so good at finding people, why didn't they ever find my father's body?"

Brooklyn's question hung in the silence between them. Minutes later, she muttered, "Just drop me off."

Shortly before nine o'clock, Holden pulled up to the curb in front of her house.

"Thanks for the ride," Brooklyn said. "I appreciate it."

Holden pushed the gearshift into park. "That's what *just-friends* are for, right?"

"I've got a lot of work to do tonight."

"Yeah, me too."

"Really?"

"No." He laughed. "Unless you need me to do some research."

"You've already helped so much." She grabbed hold of the door handle. "I'll text you tomorrow."

As she stepped out, Holden said, "Hey, Brooklyn."

"Yeah?"

"You looked beautiful tonight."

"You too."

A few steps up her driveway, Brooklyn turned back. He hadn't pulled away. She kissed her palm and blew it to him. After Holden smiled and drove off, Brooklyn tiptoed around the side yard and went in through the back door.

"Real yummy."

Taylor chewed on the succulent square of green fruit, sucking its sweet, natural juices across her taste buds.

"This new crop is the most delicious we've ever harvested," Peter enthused. "We've perfected the farming process. It's taken years, but we finally got it right."

"Very fresh." Taylor stabbed another cube with her fork. "This honeydew is *so* addictive."

"Actually, it's called Mito-Melon. We grow them right here, in that field on the south side of the compound. It's a melon, but it has been bio-engineered with an enzyme that prevents the mitochondria in a human cell from breaking down."

"Mito *what* . . . ?" Taylor asked.

"Mitochondria," he repeated slowly. "It's the part of the human cell that generates energy for all of cellular life. The problem is that over time, mitochondria break down and get damaged. This leads to the development of various diseases: diabetes, cancer, heart disease, Alzheimer's. Technically speaking, this Mito-Melon protects against what we biologists call mitochondrial deterioration and, therefore, can extend a person's life span."

He picked up a slice of the melon and held it aloft like a rare gem. "Green. There's no more beautiful color than green. It symbolizes life, fertility, freshness. A prodigious crop is a lush green. A rich forest teems with the green of biodiversity. A freshly ripened fruit or vegetable turns green before losing its youthfulness and desiccating into brown. Obviously, you've seen *Peter Pan*. What color are Peter's clothes?"

"Green."

"Indeed! The boy who doesn't want to grow old, who seeks to live in a state of perpetual youth. The boy who teaches Wendy and the Darling children how to fly. That boy from Neverland wears green because he is forever full of life. The Mito-Melon is the *green* fruit that preserves life."

The pair sat in the kitchen of Casa Bell, side by side on wooden stools at the granite counter lit by candles.

"When you complete the Program, it's like you've reached a Forever Land, a state of ageless perfection. Then you will get to choose your Forever Land name," Peter said with a glint in his eyes. "We all do it here."

"You want me to legally change my name to a *Peter Pan* name?"

"No, no, no. It's just the name fellow members call each other. It's part of the fraternity. As long as it's not already taken, you can pick anything. The only rule is that it has to come from the universe of *Peter Pan*."

Peter Pan may have been trapped in a state of endless youth, but Taylor feared she could be trapped in a state of endless hell.

Smile and nod.

"The Fruit of Youth is real." Peter pulled a thick knife from a drawer and sliced a whole melon in two. He held up each half above his head with a victor's pride. "This is the food that will fuel the next stage in the evolution of humanity. And you, my child, will be the face of it."

Taylor pretended not to notice his eyes sweeping up and down her body.

"Just look at you," he observed. "You've transformed in just a matter of days. My gosh! Already you're bio-charting closer to fifteen than your chronological sixteen. We haven't yet conducted your fitness testing or run your full blood work, but I can see your progress just by sight. You are stunning."

Taylor grew even more uncomfortable. When the back of his hand began to lightly stroke her forearm, her entire body tensed. She cleared her throat and wiggled away.

He pulled his hand off her. "Don't you find me interesting, Taylor?"

She swallowed another cube of fruit. "Of course, I do." She gulped. "You're a very, *very* brilliant man. I'm very grateful to have you as a mentor."

"That's very sweet of you." Peter looked away. "I doubt you would have felt that way when I was your age. Later stages of puberty were not very kind to me."

"It's like that for most kids." Taylor feared the dip in his emotional roller coaster would shoot back up to rage.

"My experience was far from typical. They called me a freak."

"Who did?"

"The producers, the network, the public. My parents. Everyone." He propped his elbows on the countertop and pressed his face into his hands. He rubbed his eyes. "Washed up. My acting career was over. Between fifteen and sixteen, my body just . . . well, it betrayed me, Taylor. Putrid acne dotted every inch of my face. I gained twenty-five pounds, mostly of fat. They said they didn't recognize me anymore. My mother would say, 'Oh, don't worry. God has a plan for you.' How naive, how arcane!" He machine-gun belted a series of ha-ha-ha-has. "Some God. A righteous God doesn't torture a child with changes that taint a perfect specimen. Faith is for the fools, but science is for the astute, the intelligent."

Taylor didn't dare interrupt, though she didn't quite agree with, nor entirely understand, the logic behind his bitter rant.

"But then I went to college. Got my doctorate in human biology. And now look who's getting the last laugh."

Once his lecture ended, a security guard entered and escorted Taylor, clutching a stack of study materials, across the lawn to the clinic. Two steps into her room, she stopped and propped open the door with her elbow.

"Oh no! Could you do me a favor?" she asked the guard. "I think I dropped my highlighter by the desk over there."

"Where?" the guard asked, looking down the hallway.

"It might have rolled . . ."

As he strained his eyes in the distance, Taylor spat her gum into her hand and stuck the thick pink bubble gum on the door lock. She pressed it hard.

"Don't you see it?" she added, shielding the gum-jammed door lock.

The guard took a few steps into the hallway and craned his neck. He kept walking until he got to the guard desk by the front door, some ten yards away.

"Oh, duh," she said. "It was in my pocket the whole time. Thanks for looking. Good night."

She gently shut the door. She pressed her ear against the metal and she waited. For ten minutes she listened for footsteps. He never came back. And the door never zapped into the locked position.

"Dear Brookie," began the handwritten letter Brooklyn found propped on her pillow when she returned home from L.A. "Went to bed early. Can't wait to hear all about your big night in the morning. Kisses, Mom."

Brooklyn kicked off her heels, her sore feet throbbing in their fashion freedom. She wiggled out of the dress and hung it in her closet, then put on her sweats and a T-shirt. After pulling her hair back into a tight ponytail, she sunk into the desk chair and began the process of turning all the information she had gathered about Taylor's disappearance into something she could actually publish.

She now had two anonymous sources, Beckett and Evan, telling her that Taylor had been taken against her will and she also had evidence, including video surveillance footage, suggesting virtually for certain that Taylor was taken to the Kensington Solutions property in Thermal, California. But even so, she had neither undeniable proof (the IV bag stamped "Kensington" didn't definitely place her there) nor an on-the-record source. In other words, she had a lot of dots but no official, irrefutable lines connecting any of them.

The consequences of getting her story wrong were greater than professional embarrassment. She knew that to wrongly publish a story alleging that a non-profit and its founder had essentially kidnapped a celebrity would almost certainly get her sued for libel. It could, in fact, ruin her journalism career while it was just getting started. One way to get undeniable confirmation would be with firsthand observation. But it was already past nine o'clock at night; she wasn't about to drive out to the California desert and knock on the gates of a remote compound asking for Taylor. But she could learn more by staying home and using her laptop.

She began by searching for media stories including the names Peter Kensington and Oliver Franks, and she read everything that came up about Kensington Solutions. Two hours later, Brooklyn had amassed a compelling, if also chilling portrait of a shady organization and leader that were entirely consistent with what her sources had told her. But they were dots—still unconnected.

In the Central California State University investigative journalism online training course Brooklyn had taken the previous spring, she learned that the risk of losing a defamation or libel lawsuit was significantly lower if a journalist ran a story with an on-the-record source who they believed in good faith had been telling the truth. Beckett, for whatever reason, had completely gone off the grid, and had seemed so fearful she doubted he would go on the record anyway. That left two of her sources—Simone and Evan—with whom she could make one last effort at convincing.

> Simone! Haven't heard back from you. Lets chat asap. U free?

And while Evan never replied to any previous calls or texts, and he was probably too spooked to engage on something as insecure as a phone, his cell was worth a shot.

> Great meeting today. I have an urgent question. Tell me more about Coachella Vista? And there's more . . . Plz call me.

Bed sheets. Two of them twisted ropelike and knotted together. At the end dangled a loop just big enough to tie around one's neck.

Taylor held the tangle of sheets in a bunch close to her body as she tiptoed toward her room door. She pushed the door open slowly and peered into the hallway, checking the gum that still held in the latch.

With no guard in sight, Taylor darted for the sliding doors that opened to the front courtyard. Outside there was no moon. No shadows cast beside the cactus that dotted the grounds. No coyotes howling, no German shepherds barking.

Taylor wheezed as she sprinted full-speed across the lawn. The dash in the dark seemed farther than it actually was. And it felt like a run for her life.

When she reached the stone wall, she unfurled the bed sheets. Taylor gazed at the foot-high black iron spikes that rimmed the fence top like saber-rattling soldiers. The wall seemed much higher than it had during the day. Impossibly higher.

Taylor looked back at the clinic building. No sight of a guard. While Peter's Casa Bell sat calmly in the distance, Taylor's heart beat so hard her throat pulsed with fear—and hope.

With a heave skyward, Taylor launched the thin linen rope, aiming the loop so it could lasso around a single spike. But the loop didn't catch. Instead it fell limply onto the dirt. She immediately picked it up, tossing it skyward again. This time, it secured itself around the spike. She tugged hard, anchoring it.

Taylor then sucked in a long breath, grabbed hold of the jerry-rigged rope and with all the strength she could muster, simultaneously jumped and pulled her body up. Her feet dangled as she shimmied up the rope inch by inch, grunt by grunt.

Halfway to the top, she heard a noise. She stopped moving. The sound came again. Not a taser-wielding guard. Not a trained attack dog. Not Peter catching her in the act. It was shredding. But by the time Taylor recognized the sound for what it was, she had fallen back in a free fall and landed with a thud. For a moment, she lay on her back like a corpse clutching the torn bed sheets.

Taylor struggled to her feet and dusted herself off. In a panic, she bundled the sheets in a ball, tossed the evidence of her failed escape over the wall, and made a run for it back to the clinic. Only minutes had passed, so the guard desk was still empty when she slinked back down the hallway, just as Nurse Mary had promised. And when Taylor got to the door, she saw the gum had remained stuck in place, just as Nurse Mary had suggested.

Taylor peeled it from the door, stuck it in her mouth, and swallowed. Gently closing the door, she climbed into bed, yanked the blanket over her sweaty body, and cried herself to sleep.

"BREAKING NEWS!"

Brooklyn's mouth gaped as she clicked on the giant headline on *STARSTALK*.

EXCLUSIVE: CELEB ASSISTANT FOUND DEAD IN HOTEL ROOM, SUICIDE SUSPECTED

by Giuliana Carroll | Today 10:21 PM PDT

Law enforcement sources confirm exclusively to STARSTALK that Simone Witten, the former assistant and close companion to troubled actress Taylor Prince, was found dead late Sunday night inside a room in the Beverly Hilton.

The body of Witten, who had been blamed for Prince's recent troubles with drugs that landed her in an undisclosed rehab earlier this month, was found in a bed on the seventh floor of the famed hotel. A police source said that several empty pill bottles, along with a suicide note, were found nearby.

Witten, who was 20 and whose legal name was Simone White, recently had been exclusively revealed by STARSTALK to be a two-time convicted felon for shoplifting and armed robbery. Sources have also told STARSTALK that Witten had been abusing drugs, which could have been connected to Prince's rehab stint.

Developing . . .

Brooklyn swallowed only to find her mouth had turned dry. If she had eaten dinner, she would have hurled.

She crept into the hall and made her way through the dark hallway. The layout of the house required her to walk past her mom's room on the right, then turn left through the living room in order to reach the kitchen. Halfway there, she noticed the front door was slightly cracked open.

Didn't I close it?

But Brooklyn had entered through the side door of the garage. She inched over to the door and grabbed the handle, but it jangled loosely in her hand. A screw fell to the floor. She pushed the door closed, but it wouldn't stay shut. The handle and its lock were broken.

Brooklyn twisted the deadbolt into a locking position. It worked.

She booked it back to the hallway and burst into her mom's room, locking that door behind her.

"Mom, wake up!" She panted. "Mommy!"

Her mom sprung awake in a daze. "What's the matter? What time is it?"

"I think someone may have broken into the house!"

"What the—"

"The door handle. It's busted. And so I locked it—"

"Brooklyn. It's okay. Brooklyn—"

"And I just found out about a source of mine killing herself, but I think it was these guys who killed her. At the hotel. And I was just there. That could have been me! They know I am on to them. I have to break this story before it's too late, before someone else dies—"

"Now, Brooklyn—"

"They might be after me!"

Her mom leaped to her feet and grabbed Brooklyn by the shoulders and shook her. "Brooklyn!" she shouted. "I broke the handle! It was already loose, and I turned it too hard. Uncle Don's supposed to come tomorrow to fix it. There's no burglar, no danger. Settle down. It's going to be okay."

The news sunk in, slowly. Brooklyn caught her breath.

"Everything's going to be fine," her mom said, rubbing her back.

Brooklyn leaned into her mother's chest and folded forward in a puddle of tears.

"What's going on, Brookie? Who are these people you're so afraid of?"

Brooklyn pulled out of her mother's embrace. Wiping her cheeks, she said, "I've uncovered a huge conspiracy, a story bigger than I realized. But I'm scared. I could use your help, but it's sort of . . . complicated. And I haven't been totally truthful."

"No one understands the meaning of *complicated* more than I do. And I haven't been totally truthful to you, either."

Brooklyn stepped back. "What do you mean?"

"Have a seat," her mom said. Brooklyn sat cross-legged on the edge of the bed. "It has to do with your father." Her mom began to tear up. "It's something that I've been wanting to tell you, but, quite honestly, I didn't want to upset you."

"What is it?"

Her mom exhaled. "I think your father was having an affair right before he disappeared."

"What?" Brooklyn shot to her feet. "What do you mean *think* he was? And with who?"

"I found emails after he disappeared. I can't say for certain, but his emails to this woman made it seem like there was something intimate between them."

"Who is this bitch?"

"One of his clients, someone he did security for on the weekends."

"Mom, just tell me."

"Tina Degrassi."

"The actress? That lady from the nineties? I don't believe it. No way. There's no way in hell he would do that to us, Mom. And, I mean, with that kind of . . . Wait, didn't Tina Degrassi die a few years ago?"

"Yes, she did. A few months after your father disappeared."

"Why are you just telling me this now?"

"I didn't want upset you any more, especially in those dark months after he died. And I don't know for sure if he was cheating on me with her. It's just a suspicion. But when you ran in here just now and told me about your source committing suicide, I realized I had to tell you because Tina DeGrassi also committed suicide. There's never a good time to tell your own baby such bad news, but I had to tell you now. I just did. I'm sorry it has taken me this long. I feel horrible about it. It's weighed heavily on me. I hope you can forgive me, but I don't blame you if you can't."

This was the part of the conversation when Brooklyn normally would shame her mom for not treating her like an adult, for doing the thing she hated most: keeping secrets. But she didn't. This time, she needed a teammate.

"Honestly, Mom, I've been keeping secrets from you, too."

"You mean about your event in Beverly Hills tonight?" she asked, unsurprised.

"Yeah, but also about more, about this whole investigation I have been working on."

"Well . . ." Her mom clapped her hands together. "Go ahead. We're already up!"

EXT. SUNSET:

PETER and WENDY, in a Jeep convertible, drive up a winding desert mountain road. Laughing, smiling, carefree.

Wendy turns up radio, starts singing.

WE HEAR:

For all things fresh, forever and true
Wendy sang a song for her guy,
simply called "I love you."

CUT TO:

A sign—"SCENIC OVERLOOK"

They reach the top. Peter parks the Jeep in a parking lot near the cliff's side.

WE HEAR:

I love the stars, love the moon,
love the way you make me swoon
Teach me to fly, I'll follow you high,
singing together our favorite tune

The young couple kisses before exiting the Jeep and running toward the cliff hand in hand.

"Okay. Cut!" Peter Kensington jumped from the flatbed truck that had been carting the Jeep seven miles up the steep Highway 74 to Coachella Valley Vista Point. He slapped Taylor and Evan a high five. "Perfect! Absolute perfection."

The panoramic view from the lookout atop the dusty Santa Rosa Mountains down to the Coachella Valley floor was stunningly brilliant. The flickering streetlights of Palm Springs and the rest of the desert valley stretched east, and the flat ranchlands of Thermal and the expanse of the Salton Sea, where Taylor had uncomfortably bathed with Peter, stretched west. This was her first trip outside the compound since that visit to the lake, and just as it did then, this trip brought with it much more fear than any sense of freedom.

The orange glow ringing the jagged peaks of the mountains reminded Taylor of the beauty that she hoped still waited for her after completing the Program. Back to acting. Back to family time. Back to having fun with Simone. Back to feeling normal. All the things she used to complain about—the paparazzi, the studio execs, the over-zealous fans—now seemed so trivial. She wanted her life back.

"Just look at that!" Peter stepped abruptly between Evan and Taylor, slinging his arms around both in an awkward group hug. "A perfect night for flying off a cliff, wouldn't you say?"

Taylor and Evan exchanged glances.

"Don't worry, not literally." Peter laughed. "You'll just be *simulating* a jump in our last shot. Tomorrow we'll be green-screening your leap. But first . . ."

Peter turned back to the crew of four, which consisted of George, a security guard, a lighting guy, and a camera operator, Louie. "Let's set up the last shot, *pronto*, and be ready to roll at nine sharp," he ordered Louie.

Taylor and Evan stepped up to the metal railing separating them from the canyon that angled down several hundred feet below. The chasm between them seemed just as wide.

Ever since they had reunited at the clinic last week, Taylor had been looking for signs of the charismatic guy with the boyish smile and charming personality she had fallen for just six months earlier. Even when he kissed her for the video today, Evan had seemed completely absent. He was still physically attractive, yes. But his spirit had turned hollow. And Taylor feared that, in time, the same thing might happen to her.

"So have you have picked your Program name yet?" she asked Evan. "You know, your *Peter Pan* name."

"I've given it some thought," he replied.

"Please do share. I could use some inspiration."

"You might not like what I've chosen."

"Why's that?"

"Because maybe it's a name you wanted."

"Try me."

Evan's eyes lit up. "Tinkerbell."

"Oh my god. You're kidding, right?" She giggled. "Please tell me you're kidding."

Evan let out a short laugh. "Of course I am! I was thinking 'Hook.' You know, like the captain."

"You had me worried there. For you—not me. I think I already have mine anyway, thank you very much. I'm probably going with 'Pixie.'"

"Oooh, the magical dust—excellent choice." Evan grinned. "'All the world is made of faith, and trust, and—'"

"'Pixie dust.' I've always been good at memorizing lines."

For several seconds, neither spoke. Then Taylor broke the silence. "That's the first time I've seen the old Evan in a long time."

Evan turned his neck and scanned the parking lot. "You know, maybe I'm not as out of it as I've let on."

Taylor stared into his eyes, which suddenly didn't seem so vacant.

"Everything's going to be okay," he whispered. "Just have faith."

"And trust?"

"That too."

Further along the edge of the cliff, Peter clapped his hands. "Okay, my children! Let's block out this scene."

Evan and Taylor made their way to where the camera was set up. Taylor stepped cautiously to the edge, leaning forward and looking down at the steep drop-off.

"This is the final dramatic ending," Peter said. "All this to the final lyrics."

He sang in a pitifully out-of-tune pitch:

It's a belief that can't only be sung
Fly or die, he said, gripping her hand
Lovers willing to die to achieve the state of being Forever Young!

Taylor thought the song was corny, but she didn't dare say so.

"You will take her hand, kiss each other passionately, then turn, and begin what looks like the start of a leap off the cliff. We'll shoot several angles until we get all our shots," Peter said.

George ran over to Peter, an iPad tucked under his armpit like a football. "It's that reporter girl, the one with the blog."

George handed Peter the tablet. Peter fixed his eyes on the screen for several seconds. Veins bulging across his temples, he glared at Evan. "You disloyal little brat!"

DEADLINE DIARIES EXCLUSIVE: TAYLOR PRINCE KIDNAPPED BY SECRET ANTI-AGING CULT LEADER WITH TIES TO HIGHEST LEVELS OF GOVERNMENT AND HOLLYWOOD

by Brooklyn Brant | Fri., Aug 15 | 8:45 PM PDT

A *Deadline Diaries* investigation reveals the disturbing truth behind the recent disappearance of actress Taylor Prince on her sixteenth birthday.

Contrary to reports that Prince had been admitted to a rehab to undergo treatment for substance abuse, *Deadline Diaries* has confirmed with multiple sources that, in fact, Prince was taken against her will by members of a secret anti-aging cult who, working with the help of various law enforcement and government officials, have been forcibly recruiting celebrity members through an illegal blackmail operation in order to intimidate their high-profile recruits into joining the fringe group. The alleged rehab center has been operating under the guise of a California-based non-profit known as Kensington Solutions.

Sources reveal that after apparently being drugged and taken from her home (see exclusive security video of her kidnapping here), Prince was transported via an SUV to Kensington Solutions' remote desert compound in Thermal, California, where *Deadline Diaries* has learned the actress has been confined and subjected to a grueling hazing and education ritual, possibly including electroshock therapy, which sources say is aimed at gaining the unconditional loyalty of new members.

At least one celebrity recruit has stepped forward to blow the whistle on Kensington Solutions' far-reaching conspiracy. In an exclusive interview with *Deadline Diaries,* actor Evan Ryan, widely reported to have been admitted into an undisclosed rehab earlier this year, reveals that he instead had been forced to join the Kensington group. "They call it a rehab, but it is a cult that worships youth," Ryan says. "Its goal is for its members—through a series of drug, lifestyle, and other therapies—to achieve, ultimately, what they believe is immortality. It's a twisted group that wants to sell its program to the masses. I'm lucky to still be alive."

According to Ryan, the group will typically amass negative, illegal, and damaging background information on a celebrity, often times fabricating it, and promise the celebrity they will clear their record in exchange for their dedication and lifelong enrollment in its program.

The founder and spiritual leader of the cult is Dr. Peter Kensington. Despite repeated attempts to allow him to confirm or deny any of the allegations contained in this report, *Deadline Diaries* has been unable to reach Mr. Kensington. However, our investigation has uncovered the portrait of a man with a checkered background that could shed light into his possible motivation to start his youth-obsessed celebrity cult.

- Peter Kensington's birth name is Oliver Franks, but the former child actor had it changed legally at age

18, two years after the cancellation of his sitcom, *All About Oliver,* in 1986. Media reports cited the reason for the cancellation as a precipitous drop in ratings, due in part to Kensington going through a late puberty transformation that changed his appearance.

- Kensington then attended the University of California, majoring in biology and going on to earn a PhD. He is credited with discovering in his post-doctoral research the non-lethal toxin that is the active ingredient in the popular wrinkle-erasing injectable Lovoxin, for which he holds the patent and has amassed a nearly billion-dollar fortune.

- Kensington is a major investor in scores of Hollywood business ventures, including several film production funds, a major talent agency, a public relations firm, and a TV production studio.

- Kensington Solutions holds or has applied for patents and trademarks on dozens of anti-aging products and inventions, including a bio-engineered fruit called "Mito-Melon" and a host of injectable hormones and various vitamin therapies. A source confirms that most of these products are part of a larger anti-aging lifestyle brand dubbed "the Program™."

- In what appears to be a troubling act of inhumane branding, Ryan claims that Mr. Kensington had a permanent tattoo put on both his and Taylor Prince's ankles, each with the following designs: 1^∞ and 2^∞. Explains Ryan, "He had us marked as the first two members of a newly formed elite group of celebrity recruits. She is the second, and I was the first. The infinity sign symbolized our lifetime commitment."

- In 1999, Kensington was arrested and charged with violating California Penal Code 288 for allegedly committing lewd acts on a minor under age fourteen. That child molestation case, however, was settled later that same year. Although the court records have been sealed to protect the identity of the minor, a source familiar with the 1999 case tells *Deadline Diaries* that Kensington's legal team pressured the accuser's family to recant their previous claims of child molestation. Adds the source, "With no witness, the D.A. had no choice but to drop the charges."

- In 2002, Kensington was sued for medical negligence in a San Bernardino County civil court. Although the lawsuit was later dropped by the plaintiff, *Deadline Diaries* has obtained the lawsuit and its chilling details, in which Kensington is accused of subjecting a former patient, Ronald Marrin of Palm Desert, to "repeated electroshock therapy" that left him with permanent cognitive disabilities. A source tells *Deadline Diaries* that the case was settled out of court for "over seven figures."

We were unable to reach Mr. Marrin or Mr. Kensington for comment, but Evan Ryan claims to have undergone a similar electroshock therapy at the hands of Kensington just earlier this year. "He said it was to help me heal, to cure my depression, anxiety, and addictions," Ryan says. "I fear the same could happen to Taylor."

Evan Ryan says he chose to come forward to *Deadline Diaries* rather than to law enforcement because he has well-founded suspicions that the wealthy and politically influential Mr. Kensington has several police and other high-ranking officials across the state in his pocket. Although we have yet been unable to corroborate Ryan's corruption claims, *Deadline Diaries* has learned that Kensington has donated more than $7 million dollars, often under the aegis of bogus charities or in the name of his own employees, to various elected officials over the last ten years, including the current chief of Los Angeles police and other officials.

Within the last twenty-four hours, *Deadline Diaries* has contacted L.A. police, the California state Attorney General's office, the FBI, and L.A. and San Bernardino County law enforcement officials asking whether they are aware of any potential illegal activity taking place by Kensington Solutions. None would comment on the record. But a spokesman for the FBI tells *Deadline Diaries,* "We take any and all allegations of illegal activity very seriously and will investigate any legitimate claims vigorously."

Please keep checking *DeadlineDiaries.com* for the latest updates on this developing story. . . .

—Additional reporting by Holden Lee

"You ungrateful . . ." Peter barked at Evan, his neck muscles tightening like violin strings, his face filling red with rage. "I will—"

Taylor backed away as Peter marched forward.

"Destroy me?" Evan shot back, stepping in front of Taylor. She clutched his hips and hid behind him.

Towering over him, Evan poked Peter in the chest. "You've already destroyed me; you're not hurting her. You little sicko. You. Are. Done!" Evan's pokes turned into violent, two-handed pushes. "You're nothing but a sad, little, evil, *old* man!"

Before Evan could finish him off with a slug, a thundering *thwap-thwap* of whipped air and dust enveloped the cliff top. All eyes shot skyward at a helicopter as a spotlight shone down, tracing a circle on the ground around Peter.

Taylor grabbed Evan's hand and ran toward a convoy of police cruisers and SWAT vans that squealed into the parking lot.

Within seconds, dozens of gun barrels pointed at the thin man in the seersucker suit who had been chasing his dream of forever but now faced a nightmare of an end.

Taylor pulled Evan behind the cavalry of cops and rifle marksmen shouting at the scientist over the roar of the helicopter blades.

Hands up! On your knees!

Peter ignored their orders. He shuffled closer toward the edge, bent over and scooped up as much dust as he could hold in each of his tiny hands. Inching closer to the drop-off, he tossed the dust into the air, watching it dissipate into a swirl of nothingness.

Although an array of red laser sights fixed on his back, no

bullets would be needed. Peter spread his arms to his sides and sprang into a headfirst dive over the cliff, disappearing into the darkness below. His last sound of life was a distant, rocky thud.

This Peter couldn't fly, and he would never find forever.

Sunday service. Not long ago Brooklyn Brant had insisted she wouldn't be caught dead in St. Francis Catholic Church on a Sunday. But that was before she had chased a deadline that turned deadly. Before two sources—Simone and Beckett—were murdered. Before the primary focus of her investigation leaped to his death. Before she had gone from being regarded as the loner blogger-girl and object of Twin Oaks pity, to achieving the kind of hometown hero status befitting the daughter of the city's most hallowed fallen hero. Before she and her mom had obliterated the walls of secrets between them and grown closer, though the mystery surrounding her father's last days, and his death, remained an obsession for Brooklyn. But now was a time to give thanks.

Those previous evenings of Saturday Mass solitude also came before her groundbreaking report on what the media had come to call the "Coachella Cult." It dominated the mainstream media and elevated Brooklyn from "teen celebrity blogger" to "investigative journalist." Brooklyn's investigation, including the several follow-up reports that revealed the entire scope of Peter Kensington's twisted pursuits, set off an aftershock of arrests, media scandals, and sweeping investigations, among them:

- The arrest of the Kensington Clinic staff on charges ranging from kidnapping to child abuse
- An ongoing FBI investigation into the apparent murders of Simone Witten and Beckett Collins
- A grand jury probe into the alleged bribery scandal involving a half-dozen politicians and law enforcement personnel with personal and financial ties to Kensington

- The forced resignation of Mayor Luis Suarez for directing court and police officials to fabricate cases against innocent celebrities
- The firing of *STARSTALK*'s editor Emily Lamont, who had received millions of dollars in bribes from Peter Kensington in exchange for publishing false stories he requested
- A California Attorney General investigation into possible crimes committed by Superior Court Judge Ronald Opin and employees and executives of Hollywood production companies, law and publicity firms, and talent agencies who knowingly assisted Peter Kensington's illegal activity

To Brooklyn's left sat Holden, who had begun going to church with Brooklyn, if only to thank God for not letting either of them get hurt while investigating. Brooklyn smiled as she held hands with her mother to her right, who had provided just enough assistance in the form of legal research to give Brooklyn the confidence to publish her initial report.

Upon learning of the illegal activity her daughter had uncovered, her mom had vetted the story for any legal problems on the condition that Brooklyn had to directly tip off law enforcement about the Coachella Vista video shoot, which led to the raid.

Several days later, Taylor Prince reached out with a phone call to thank Brooklyn for saving her. She had invited Brooklyn to come down to L.A. and hang out—maybe they could get to know each other and be friends—but Brooklyn graciously declined.

"The worst thing a journalist can do is become part of the story," Brooklyn explained. "I was just doing my job."

"You know," Taylor said, "I never really appreciated celebrity journalists as real journalists. Sure, they publicized my projects, informed fans about my comings and goings, kept me in the public eye. But the media mostly really just bugged me. I always thought they were a necessary evil. Like agents."

"Reporters are a necessary evil because there is evil that needs to be exposed."

Brooklyn had once fantasized about meeting Taylor. Yet over the last few weeks Brooklyn had fully transformed from a fan-blogger into a full-fledged reporter. "Thanks for the offer to hang out, but between school and my blog, I'm pretty busy."

"I understand," Taylor said. "But can I ask you something?"

"Of course."

"When I was away, did Simone say anything I should know?"

Brooklyn considered the question. "She told me that if you weren't an actress, you wanted to be a journalist, which I thought was pretty cool."

Taylor sighed. "Yeah, I guess being on the other side gave me an appreciation for the power of the pen—for good and bad. I doubt I will ever be a journalist, but with your permission, I would like to play one."

"You don't need my permission for that."

"Actually, I do."

"Why?"

"Because I want to play *you*! I want to produce and star in a movie about the uncovering of the Coachella Cult."

"Seriously?"

"Totally being serious!" Taylor said. "I can't think of a more important story to tell. Of course, I'd pay you for the rights."

Stunned, Brooklyn felt as if she were in a movie starring herself.

"And I already have a title: *Finding Forever*."

"That's pretty cool," Brooklyn said. "I'd be honored."

"I've been wanting to ask you . . ." Taylor's tone turned serious. "Is there anything else you can tell me about Simone, anything she said or did before she died?"

Brooklyn paused to think. "Actually, she said she felt guilty about not protecting you better the night of your birthday party."

"It wasn't her fault," Taylor said. "I was the one who insisted on not having security. I wish I could do that whole night over again."

That call between Taylor and Brooklyn had happened almost two weeks ago. Brooklyn now sat listening to Father McGavin, just as she always had. She felt a sense of peace and calm she hadn't experienced since her father's death. But she didn't feel total closure. Brooklyn prayed for the loved ones of those who died.

"There is life after death," Father McGavin said. "And it is forever. It never stops. Death marks a new beginning."

Brooklyn also felt that the end of the Taylor Prince investigation signaled a beginning for her.

As the congregation stood and sang its closing hymn, Brooklyn looked forward to getting back and checking her *Deadline Diaries* email inbox, which was now filled with tips from sources sharing click-worthy Hollywood news, misdeeds, frauds, and scandals. And Brooklyn couldn't wait to shine her light of truth on as many of them as her growing journalistic confidence—and faith—gave her the inspiration to investigate.

ACKNOWLEDGMENTS

Legendary college basketball coach John Wooden once said: "I think the teaching profession contributes more to the future of our society than any other single profession." My personal experience confirms this to be true.

As such, I want to express my gratitude to some especially influential mentors who shaped my future during my undergraduate days at Colgate University: Walt Shepperd for giving me my first on-the-job training in investigative journalism at the *Syracuse New Times*, English professor Don Snyder for inspiring me to envision a writing life after hockey, sage Gary Ross for his wise advice, my hockey coaches Terry Slater (RIP) and Brian Durocher for believing in me, and New Hampshire pilgrim John Friberg for being a superb academic role model to this dumb jock.

Back in 1994, the Columbia University Graduate School of Journalism's MVP Sam Freedman, also an accomplished author, told me, "There's no such thing as 'writer's block.'" This book, as well as my others, may never have been completed on time if I hadn't repeated Sam's sentence mantra-like to myself as I stared at a blank computer screen.

To every teacher out there helping a young writer find their voice, I thank you for waging the front-line battle to ensure a future where storytelling exists in more than 140 characters.

I have learned something valuable from every good, bad, and so-so teacher I have ever had, including my fifth grade teacher, Mrs. McGraw, who frequently made me stand in a corner for talking too much (*E! News* viewers know that lesson clearly didn't stick).

But teachers don't just exist inside classrooms. In their unconditional love of life, hockey, and their dad (not necessarily in that order), Jackson and Chloe teach me so much about the power of positivity. My mother's passion for reading and my father's unrealized passion for writing impacted me in subtle yet profound ways.

I am appreciative of my longtime editor at Running Press, Lisa Cheng, for allowing me to be a student in her How to Write Fiction class. In creating yet another brilliant cover, RP's Teresa Bonaddio has taught me to leave cover art design to a pro. Similar kudos to Valerie Howlett, Seta Zink, and the rest of my Running Press posse.

To lit agent extraordinaire Michael Bourret, and Ashley Mills and her team at CAA, you are all my Ari Golds (minus the diva behavior, of course).

Without my *E! News* and *E! Online* family providing me a front row seat to celebrity theatre and a daily platform to spew on-air monologues about all things Hollywood, I would not have the inspiration to write the *Deadline Diaries* series.

I haven't forgotten about you, the reader. I am forever grateful that book after book you have been there for me . . . and are never shy about tagging @kenbakernow on social media.

Finally, a note of appreciation goes to the real star of this book show, Brooklyn Brant. Like all great characters, both real and imagined, I didn't find you as much as you found me. Thanks for reminding me (and hopefully teaching others) why a journalism career is such a privileged and worthy adventure on which to embark.

Ken Baker is an E! News Correspondent. He is the author of *How I Got Skinny, Famous, and Fell Madly in Love* and *Fangirl*, and his memoir, *Man Made: A Memoir of My Body*, is the inspiration for the upcoming film *The Late Bloomer*. He lives (and writes) with his family in Hermosa Beach, CA. You can follow him on Twitter, Instagram, and Snapchat @kenbakernow.